"The Pameroy mysteries never disappoint! I love how history gets mixed into the present. After reading this book, I really feel like I know Lillia and her Grauntie. Great read. Can't wait for the next!"

"What a fun mystery! I feel like I am right there with Lillia and Charlie during their adventures. Humorous, lighthearted and quite a page turner! I will definitely be recommending this one every chance I get!"

"Drawn into this book right from the beginning! My thirteen-year-old niece has read both books in this series and loved them. So, it's been nice that we've both enjoyed and can chat about them! Great read not just for tweens."

WATCHED PLACES

A PAMEROY MYSTERY

BRENDA FELBER

ISBN-13:978-0-9909092-2-4 paperback

ISBN-13:978-0-9909092-3-1 eBook

Cover design by eBook Launch

Publisher's Cataloging-in-Publication data

Names: Felber, Brenda, author.

Title: Watched places : a Pameroy mystery / Brenda Felber.

Series: Pameroy mystery.

Description: Schofield, WI: Laughing Deer Press, 2016

Identifiers: ISBN 978-0-9909092-2-4 (pbk.) | 978-0-9909092-3-1 (ebook)

Summary: The ghost of a pirate queen threatens the life of Lillia Pameroy's brother. Lillia

must reach the buried treasure site in time to save Charlie.

Subjects: LCSH LCSH Friendship--Juvenile fiction. | Family--Juvenile fiction. | Psychics--Juvenile fiction. | Alabama--Bon Secour Bay--Juvenile fiction. | Pirates—Alabama--History--Juvenile fiction. | Mothers and sons--Juvenile fiction. | Ghosts--Juvenile fiction. | Ghost stories. | Imaginary playmates--Juvenile fiction. | Mystery fiction. | BISAC JUVENILE

FICTION / Mysteries & Detective Stories | JUVENILE FICTION / Horror & Ghost Stories | JUVENILE FICTION / Paranormal, Occult & Supernatural

Classification: LCC PZ7.F33375 Wa 2016 | DDC [Fic]--dc23

CONTENTS

QUOTE TO PONDER...

"Now and then we had a hope that if we lived and were good, God would permit us to be pirates."

Mark Twain, *Life on the Mississippi*

1

LILLIA

I hope you visit Bon Secour someday and tour the historic Swift family home. Maybe then you'll believe what happened to me there. Maybe you'll feel what I felt when I first saw the old mansion in the dark of night. Something was astir here. The veil that hides the past was maybe just a little thinner in this place.

"Please join us. We have been watching for you," said a girl seated at a small round table. She reached across to hand me a tightly folded piece of paper. "This note is for you. Refrain from opening it now, as we have work to do."

Across the table from her, a blindfolded girl turned her face in my direction, moving her head side to side, as though trying to see through the white fabric tied over her eyes. She asked, "Miriam, who are you talking to?"

"Shush Nell. Keep your attention on the board and no peeking," scolded Miriam. "Lillia Pameroy, approach slowly and willingly. You must believe the truth of Ouija or leave immediately."

Giggles escaped from two other girls I saw standing in the shadows outside of the low candle light. "I'm Eleanor and this is Emily." Eleanor moved to make room for me near the table. "Nell is the youngest of us four Swift sisters. She is the best at the Ouija board. I can't blame her for peeking. I think I would too."

"Thank you, sister." Nell's smile beamed beneath the blindfold.

"Eleanor! Stop this minute. You'll break the spell. I can almost feel him. He'll be here soon." Miriam took a deep cleansing breath and did a dramatic shoulder roll. "So, are we ready now?"

The girls, in their old-fashioned long white nightgowns, nodded solemnly. Miriam looked at me. I, in my t-shirt and pajama bottoms, nodded too, letting her know I was ready. Not sure what I was ready for, but here we go.

Miriam and Nell's fingertips hovered above a small triangular object with short stubby legs. It rested on a wooden board covered in writings and designs.

Closing her eyes, Miriam said, in a solemn voice, "We welcome you Laurens de Graaf. Lillia Pameroy is now with us." She and Nell gently placed their fingertips on the three-sided planchette. "Let the communications to the spirit of Laurens de Graaf be opened."

The air grew chilly. I held my breath.

Then slowly, turning in random, uneven, gliding slides, the planchette began moving. Nell's and Miriam's fingers, barely touching the piece, followed its disjointed moves. The three of us standing, leaned in closer...mesmerized.

It stopped.

"What does it say? Where did it stop?" Nell asked.

"Hush Nell," Miriam said.

Eleanor stretched out, tilting her head to see. "It stopped over the word *HELLO*."

In a serious, no nonsense tone, Miriam said, "Hello. Is this the pirate Laurens de Graaf?"

The planchette started a tiny circular movement. The circling widened. Miriam and Nell's arms reached and bent as they followed it moving across the board.

Suddenly it stopped again.

A gasp rose from Eleanor. "It's on *YES*."

Emily did a silent little clap-clap motion.

I leaned over to Emily and asked, "Who's Laurens de Graaf?"

"Silence," Miriam commanded.

Emily whispered in my ear, "Only the cutest pirate who ever lived here or anywhere."

Miriam sent another glare our way, which I noted isn't easy to do with your eyes closed, before asking, "Are you tall and blonde like in the drawing?"

The planchette did some slow zigzag movements. Then quickly shot back and stopped once more on the YES.

The girls gave little squeals.

"Tell us something that shows you are truly him," Nell blurted out.

The planchette spun sharply to point to the word NO. Before anyone could ask another question, the movement started again, catching Miriam and Nell by surprise. It darted quickly around the board, stopping at letters just long enough for someone to call them out.

L I L L I A H E L P M Y P I R A T E Q U E E N A N N E

Emily and Eleanor looked at me with questioning eyes. In a low voice, speaking as quietly as I could, so as not to upset Miriam, I said, "Ask how."

Miriam cleared her throat and said, "How can Lillia help her?"

T O C O M E H O M E T O M E

The planchette darted to *GOODBYE.*

Nell's blindfold dropped off and I saw her wide-eyed expression. "We did it. We did it. We talked to Laurens de Graaf. But wait, how can we be sure this was him?"

Miriam said, "I am sure."

Eleanor rolled her eyes. "How?"

"He said her name was Anne. I read that Laurens was married to a lady privateer named Anne Dieu-le-Veut."

Eleanor said, "You could have just moved the planchette around to stop where you wanted it to. You knew her name was Anne. You peeked and moved over those letters!"

"I am the oldest and I would not do that. How dare you question my honor?"

"Emily, did you see her peek? Or Nell what about you?"

Nell said, "I did not move it. Cross my heart and hope to die."

I heard the squabbling continue even as the girls faded from sight, leaving me alone in the room. I shook my head to clear my thoughts. I had just been with sisters who had lived in here, right in this house. By the looks of their clothes it must have been long ago. The imaginings were starting.

I remembered the note Miriam had handed me. Clicking on my small flashlight, I lifted the beam to shine on the paper. Written in a very neat cursive script, ten times nicer than mine, I read…

Lost to her complete madness,

I saw it on her face.
Touched by the greatest sadness,
She stayed in the dark black place.

Lillia is the imagineer,
With enough strength and might,
To help the watcher hear,
The words to make things right.

Please help,
Laurens de Graaf

Wait! This reminded me of something. I hurried back to our little apartment and pulled another note out of my suitcase. My spirit guide in Kentucky had given it to me before I left.

I read…

In a place called Bon Secour,
The story has been told,
Of a pirate ship on shore,
And the theft of more than gold.

You are the one imagineer,
With enough strength and might,

Watched Places

> *To help the watcher hear,*
> *The words to make things right.*

> *I know you can help in Bon Secour,*
> *Best wishes,*
> *Your guide,*
> *Emily*

I laid the papers side by side. The last verses were almost identical. Now I knew I was in the right place.

2

LATE NIGHT ARRIVAL

T he day had started out with engine problems and a
flight delay. Eight hours after meeting at the Kansas
airport, Nora, Lillia and Charlie landed in Mobile. They
were met by Nora's friend, Myra Barker. The group piled
into Myra's car and set out on the drive to the old mansion,
home for the next few days.

"Ta da! Here it is. The Swift-Coles Historic Home! Y'all
are going to be the only ones here until the docents show up
tomorrow morning. It'll be bustling then," Myra said as she
pulled into the stone drive and drove slowly around the big
white mansion. "I'm going to drop you off in the rear. You
can unload your luggage and carry your things right on in."

She parked the car, leaving the headlights on to light the
path to the back entrance.

Nora got out and stretched. "Whew! What a day. Plane
ride wasn't too bad, but that delay took it out of me. Sorry

old friend that I've put you out having to pick us up at such a late hour."

"No problem! I'm so grateful you're able to come help." Myra unloaded their suitcases. "Here you go kids, take these right in through that back door and upstairs to the apartment."

"I'm so excited to finally get to see the place after so many years of your hard work. How long has it been? Ten years since I've visited?"

"What the...," Charlie blurted out as he tripped over something. His suitcase flew out of his hand and popped open, spilling his clothes out on the ground.

Lillia, right behind him, caught herself before she fell too.

"Are you all right? What happened?" Myra scurried up and reached out to Charlie. "Goodness! I should have turned on some more lights before I let you out. Hang on now y'all and I'll run turn lights on."

Charlie moved so he could see what he had tripped over. A statue stared straight up at him with blank eyes. A shiver ran through Charlie as he watched the statue's small straight mouth turn up slightly.

Hey, had that statue smiled? Charlie scrambled to push his things back into the suitcase and hurried up the path. He was not at all excited to be staying in this old place with its creepy statues. A bright light blinded him. He stopped in his tracks.

Lillia walked right into him. "Charlie! I almost fell over you twice now…quit getting in my way."

"Sorry…I didn't mean to."

Nora passed both of them lugging her luggage. "Come along now you two. Let's get inside."

Myra held the back door open for them. "I don't know why the motion detector lights didn't turn on. But then again no one comes here at night anymore. I'll have the handyman check those out. Think you'll be comfortable with the alarm off tonight?"

"Absolutely! We'll be fine. Far as I'm concerned leave it off all the while we're here. I wouldn't want Charlie sleep-walking and setting the motion detectors off," Grauntie Nora said, patting the top of Charlie's head.

He groaned and ducked away. "Aw, come on. I don't sleepwalk that often."

Lillia said, "How would you know? You're asleep when you're doing it."

Myra said, "I'm glad it's all right with you, because now the ghosts can get out and play a little too! Hate when they trigger the alarm."

"Ghosts? Grauntie, she's kidding, right? I mean, ah… that would be cool…not that I'm afraid of them or anything." Charlie stumbled over his words.

"Don't worry, I brought you your own little flashlight," Nora whispered into her grandnephew's ear. He glanced up at her with gratitude in his eyes.

"Here you go," Myra said, opening a second-floor door

and flipping a switch. "This will be your home for the next few days. It was a small apartment for the previous owner while he restored the mansion."

"This is great. Thank you for your hospitality Myra."

"I appreciate you helping out the next few days."

"I'm seeing lots of progress since I was here last," Nora said.

"We try. Funds go fast keeping up a big house like this," Myra said as she showed Nora around. "And now with our restoring the grounds the money goes twice as fast. We do the best we can. So much glorious southern history here, can't let it slip into disrepair and ruin."

Nora said, "And knowing the South, the Kudzu vines would love to take over and gobble the house up."

Myra laughed. "You've got that right. Here, let me show you the rest of what you'll need for your stay."

The door across the room caught Charlie's eye. Its glass reflected the room he stood in. Charlie couldn't see what was outside in the dark. Anybody could be looking in at him.

"What's out that door?" he asked.

"It goes out to the upper verandah on the front of the house. Y'all can use it anytime. I'm off now. See you in the morning," Myra said.

Charlie pressed his face against the glass door, peering into the blackness of the rural setting. "Sure is dark out there."

3

LILLIA

I told Charlie, "Dah! That usually happens at night. It gets dark." Then opening the door, I stepped outside to the upper verandah.

I watched Myra's car pull around, its headlight beams sweeping across the scene below me. The beams straightened and pointed down the old road. Her red taillights faded away between the trees.

A fog horn blew its lonely, melancholy notes out in the darkness. Huge tree branches reached across the grounds. The moon shadows they cast blurred the paths and statues beneath them.

A shiver went through me as a cool breeze brushed past. The mugginess of the air pushed the chill deeper into me. I couldn't shake the feeling that we were not alone here tonight.

From the moment we had arrived, I felt as though I was

being watched. Like something or someone waited for me. I was sure that I'd seen a burning candle in an upstairs window when we first drove up. Myra said it wasn't possible. That it must have been a reflection.

Back inside the small apartment, Charlie had blown up the air mattress. Grauntie was feathering our nest, getting out pillows and blankets.

She set her digital photo frame on the kitchen counter and plugged it in. She always brought it on trips, unless we didn't have electricity like that time we camped out in the woods. The frame was stocked with memories caught by her camera. I loved it and soon fell asleep watching the parade of memories flip by.

Something woke me. It took me a minute to remember where I was. The light from the photos passing by in the frame lit the room. Charlie, now asleep on his air mattress, his blankets piled in a bundle at his feet. He had moved closer to Grauntie's door, probably because of his fear of the dark I thought.

The chimes of a clock somewhere in the big house ended.

Maybe those chimes woke me? I sank back down into the couch cushions and pulled my blanket around me, tight up under my chin. The photo, passing by in the frame, showed Zoe and me heading out to fish on Kentucky Lake. Just as I sensed sleep was coming back, I heard noises again.

I lay still, quiet, waiting. Murmuring voices came from somewhere inside the house.

BRENDA FELBER

With a small flashlight in hand, I had stepped out of our little nest and into the big house to explore.

And that's when I discovered the girls in the room with the candle. I just knew I shouldn't have doubted myself about that candle!

4

FIRST MORNING

Nora sat sipping her morning coffee in a chair on the verandah. She had to chuckle thinking of how she'd almost tripped over Charlie and his air mattress huddling against her bedroom door.

"Morning," Lillia mumbled as she walked out, rubbing the sleep from her eyes.

"Morning sweetie. How'd you sleep? You look tired. Yesterday was a long day for us. Nice to be settled in here."

"It sure was a long day." Lillia leaned on the railing, gazing out over the lawns. "Wow, those trees are huge!"

Nora said," Southern live oaks. Look like they'd make perfect climbing trees for you two. I have to believe that all eleven of the Swift children climbed in those very trees. And before them, children of the local fishermen played in them. Much earlier the trees probably had Creek Indian boys and girls crawling out on their strong branches. What those limbs have seen!"

"What is that dead stuff dangling from them?"

"It's called Spanish moss and is actually a living plant that has flowers."

"I don't see flowers. Just grayish, greenish, twisty, kinky, tangled, scrubby thingies hanging over the branches."

Nora threw back her head and laughed out loud. "Guess that's as good of a description as any I've heard."

"I can't believe how many statues are around here. It must have been so pretty when everything was new and flowering," Lillia said.

"It is still beautiful. Thank goodness for people like Nik Coles. He restored this property before donating it to the Baldwin County Historical Society."

"What are you going to do here Grauntie?"

"I'm here to help the volunteers give tours. Imagine all the history. You like old things, so I bet you'll enjoy this place."

Lillia turned to see her brother peering out the door to the porch. "Sleep-a-long-time Charlie's up! Hope he didn't sleepwalk again, like that time in the campground when he almost walked off a cliff."

"Hey, I never hurt myself," Charlie said. "Can I have some cereal?"

"Nope. Since everyone's up let's head over to the Tin Roof."

"First-morning ice cream! Yah!" He spun quickly, running back inside to get dressed.

Grauntie called after him to brush his teeth and comb his hair.

* * *

The Tin Roof Restaurant was a short walking distance away. It was a low-slung building with a large covered patio to one side. Picnic tables filled the roofed outdoor space. Plastic sheeting hung in rolls under the roof line, ready to be dropped to protect diners from wind or rain.

Pieces of conversations, dishes clattering in wash pans, chairs scraping on tile floors, and spoons clinking against sides of cups saturated the interior with background noise as Lillia, Charlie, and Nora entered.

The layered smells of pancakes with warm maple syrup, bacon freshly fried, and coffee aroma rising from squat glass pots surrounded them as they waited for a table.

Behind the cash register, a waitress was ringing out a customer. She glanced up quickly and said, "Be right with you folks."

Nora winked at Charlie and Lillia before saying, in a loud voice, "We've been waiting here forever."

The waitress grabbed three menus and scurried around the counter before she took a good look at who was complaining. Then with a big hoot, she said, "Oh my, aren't you a sight for sore eyes! Welcome back to Alabama old friend."

She gave Nora a hug and said, "I didn't know you were going to be here. When did you get in? Where are you staying?"

"Myra needed help for a few days at the big house and I was happy to come out. We're staying in the old apartment there."

"And who are these two handsome youngin's?"

"Cecelia, I'd like you to meet my grandniece Lillia and my grandnephew Charlie."

"Sure is nice to meet you two. Traveling with your grandaunt? Bet she keeps you hopping."

Charlie said, "Hi. Grauntie said you have good food here. We do ice cream for our first breakfast."

Cecelia let out a big laugh, slapped her hands against her wide hips and said, "Well I'll be. He's just like his daddy, always after them sweets! Some for you too young lady?"

Lillia smiled and said, "Sure."

"You call her Grauntie, now isn't that just the cutest thing? Kinda smooshed grand and aunt together? I love it! Come on in y'all and have a seat and I'll be over to take that ice cream order. Flavors right up there," Cecelia said, pointing to a chalkboard behind the diner's counter.

"So Daddy came here with Grandpa and Grandma when he was little?" Lillia asked.

"Right, and I'd tag along. You know me, always up for

travel. We'd stay in one of the fishing cottages on the Bon Secour River. Such fun times. Little old row boat came with the place. Spent the days fishing and crabbing. Fires in the stone fire pit at night. And we'd drive out to the Gulf of Mexico one day and spend it on the beach."

"Fishing?" Charlie asked.

"Beach?" Lillia chimed in.

5

LILLIA

I would love to see the beaches here. Waves crashing. Warm sand between my toes. Gulls flying and calling out overhead. I could only imagine.

"Fishing we can make happen, getting to the beach I'm not so sure about. I don't have a car and it's a bit of a ride," Grauntie said.

I said, "It's okay if you can't." I knew I was looking for any excuse to get out of helping this watcher. Who was Laurens, the pirate guy, anyway? I didn't have much self-confidence as far as my special abilities went.

Then I remembered how good it felt to solve the mystery in Land Between the Lakes. It had given me my first real sense of my imagining abilities, made me feel better about myself.

Cecelia showed us to a table against a wall showcasing

photographs of boats, along with pelicans, sunsets, and fisherman holding up humongous catches. A local artist had done the photography. Her work showed just how much she loved this area. Like the photos in Grauntie's frame showed her love for her travels and her family.

Large paper placements, with ads from the local fish market, dry cleaner, pirate boat cruise, funeral home, and fishing excursions, sat atop red and white checkered tablecloths. Salt and pepper shakers, ketchup, hot sauce, and a strong wire stand with napkins gathered in the center of the table.

Our wooden chairs had that slightly sticky surface that builds up over years of use. The legs were nicked and scruffy. My chair did a little teeter totter when I sat down.

Charlie's chair legs must have been more uneven because he started rocking his chair as soon as he sat on it. Back and forth. Tip tap tip.

"Knock it off! That is so annoying," I said.

Grauntie, draped her arm across the back of his chair to stop him and asked, "Now which flavor of ice cream would you like?"

Cecelia reached in her apron pocket and pulled out her order pad, pen in hand. "I have a suggestion for y'all. We do tasty breakfast waffles, so how's about I put your ice cream scoop on top of one of those? I could add hot chocolate too if you want."

"Hmm...sounds yummy. And coffee for me please,"

Grauntie said. Cecelia turned and grabbed a cup from a nearby rack and flagged over a waitress with a coffee pot in hand.

I ordered my ice cream on a warm waffle. So did Charlie.

Looking over the placemat advertisements, Charlie said, "Hey check out this Pirate Boat Cruise."

Cradling her coffee mug with her hands, Grauntie said, "Boat cruise?"

"It says Captain Jack makes the history of pirates come alive. So maybe there's buried pirate treasure here?" Charlie looked up from ads, and asked, "Lillia, how much do a pirate earrings cost?"

I shrugged.

"A buccaneer. What do pirates use to clean up a mess?"

Before I even had a chance to think, Charlie quickly said, "A sea sponge."

Oh great, he's on a pirate joke kick now. I tried to ignore him by turning to glance around the diner. A family of three were seated by the front window. Next table over, an elderly woman with strong gray streaks in her faded red hair caught me looking and nodded. I nodded back before awkwardly shifting my eyes. Nearby a couple of older men were deep in conversation, each taking turns shoving in large bites of food while the other one talked. At the counter a man sat reading a newspaper.

A plate filled with a steaming waffle and topped with a

mound of butter pecan ice cream appeared in front of me. Yum!

The ice cream melted into the small perfect squares of the golden brown waffle. I poured warm gooey maple syrup on top, watching it cut rivulets in the white mounds before dripping off the plate. I swiped my fingers around to catch the syrupy melt, then licked them off.

Cecelia pulled up a chair next to us and sat down, her wide bottom hanging over the edges. "So Nora, how's Adam doing? He done cooked up two beautiful children, that's for sure."

"My family is going to have another baby soon," Charlie blurted out, with ice cream running down his chin.

"Well, now isn't that grand? Boy or girl?"

"We don't know yet. I had a twin sister who died, so a girl would be nice for Mommy. But me, I'd like a brother."

Pulling back to take a good look at Charlie, Cecelia said, "You don't say. I'm right sorry. That's about the saddest thing I've heard in a long time. How old was she when you lost her?"

"She died before she was born," Charlie answered. "So zero? But sometimes I remember her. I dream she is with me and we can do things together. I know it's not real, though. Everyone says don't be sad Charlie, but Mom and Dad are still sad."

Cecelia gave Charlie a hug, holding him against her full rounded chest while he held his spoon upright out of harm's way. "Don't none of us really understand those kinds of things, Charlie. And you feel sad if you need too. I know she's a sweet angel and is watching you. I'll just bet she visits with you. After all, you did get to meet her before she passed. You're the only one who did. Not a one of us knows everything for real and for sure."

I was blown away hearing her talk so grown up like that to Charlie. Wish Mom and Dad could hear this. Maybe Mom wouldn't blame me for what happened over eight years ago. Maybe she wouldn't be afraid of me.

"Tell you what my little man, I've got my grandson Matt living with me. He's about your age I reckon. How's about the two of you getting together while you're here?"

"Why Cecelia, what an excellent idea," Grauntie Nora said. "Why not send him over to the big house today? Perhaps the boys would like to take a guided tour of the mansion?"

I have to admit I agreed with Charlie when he said, "Ah, not sure if a tour of an old house would be something he would like to do."

"Oh, now you never mind about if he wants to take it or not. It would do him good. And Charlie, I'll send some of our fishing' poles along in case you decide not to take the tour," Cecelia said. "Just watch out for gators. I hear a big one named Old Boy hangs round that School House creek, near the old pond."

Charlie's eyes slowly grew huge and bug like. "Gators? Like alligators? Do they bite?"

Calm as can be, Cecelia said," Not much, especially you don't bite them first."

Too funny! I watched Charlie get the joke a beat behind me. I liked Cecelia.

6

OPEN FOR TOURS

Whether it was the scents of gardenias and magnolias from a sun-filled garden, or the soft roll of words from a southern drawl, Nora wasn't sure what lured her to feel so relaxed in the South. Maybe images like that of a lady on a porch swing, beads of moisture sliding down the side of her iced tea glass, leisurely moving her fan near her arched neck caused it? Maybe the ancient rhythm of the tides on the sandy, white beaches? Nora thought a moment more, than decided she'd not concern herself with what caused it. She just decided to enjoy the I-have-all-the-time-in-the-world feeling.

Nora thought about Cecelia's surprised look earlier. She's such a sweetie. And what nice things she said to Charlie about Chloe. Nora knew the whole family struggled with losing her. She hoped Cecelia's grandson shows up to keep Charlie entertained. Lillia did well in old places like this house, but Charlie might get bored pretty quickly.

The Swift-Coles house would soon open for the first tour group. Tourists had already gathered. Nora peeked out and saw that a few were seated on the benches set up in the shade of the expansive front verandah. Some strolled the grounds, enjoying the beautiful yard statues and admiring the refurbishing being done to the gardens.

"Nora, did you get a chance to go over the refresher notes for the tour?" Myra asked as she straightened the literature about the area on the front hall entry table. "Hopefully, you can handle an afternoon tour on your own."

"How's this? Welcome to the Swift-Coles Historic Home. Built by the lumberman, Charles Swift, as an addition to the smaller dogtrot style home of Thomas Gavin. It is an excellent example of a tidewater mansion from the early 1900s."

Myra laughed and hugged Nora. "I knew I could count on you! Quiz. What is the name of the young boy whose blue coat is lying on the bed upstairs?"

"Ira Swift. After attending West Point, he became a brigadier general."

"How many children did the Swift's have?"

"Eleven."

"Very good Grauntie! I'm impressed," Lillia said.

"Can you image keeping them in clothes?" Myra held up a book titled *Food, Fun, and Fable.* "Which of the children eventually opened a famous restaurant, Nora?"

"Amelia. The restaurant was called Meme's. Did I tell you the weird happening in Kentucky? One of Meme's old menus showed up."

"My goodness no you didn't. How very odd," Myra said. "I love those great big small world stories."

Lillia asked, "Myra, is it all right if I follow along on the tour?"

"Of course, happy to have you." And with that, Myra opened the front door saying, "Welcome y'all to the Swift-Coles Historic Home. I'm excited to share with you this excellent example of a tidewater mansion from the early 1900's. I will try to make its history come alive for you on our tour."

The group followed Myra as she waved them into the large central hall. She explained that the Swift family had added on to the home of a Creole fisherman and his family. She pointed out the soft pine horizontal lumber of the original dogtrot style home buried inside the current home.

Myra continued, "Mrs. Swift kept her extensive library of books in this grand hall. She considered the education of her children, all eleven of them, to be of utmost importance."

She then led her group into the parlor. She pointed to a room with a velvet rope across the door, saying, "This room contains antiques from around the world, including from France, Greece and Spain. We like to believe that the spirits of Europeans contained in these pieces are enjoying our southern hospitality." The group chuckled politely.

Myra explained how the home was purchased by a local restauranteur named Nik Coles after the death of the last Swift to live here, Susan Nell Swift Marshall.

7

LILLIA

I smiled as I remembered the blindfolded girl from last night, little Nell. So she was the last Swift family member to live here.

We moved up the staircase to the second floor hall.

A teenage girl tripped and stumbled on the last step, dropping her cell phone. I muffled a giggle because Myra had just pointed out the shallower step, calling it the Swift's security system.

I hope I never did something like that. How embarrassing. She must have been texting and not paying attention. A small woman patted her arm and bend to pick up the teen's phone. The woman seemed familiar to me, but moved aside before I got a good chance to see her.

Myra saved the girl further embarrassment by saying, "I've got a feeling you did that on purpose to show what could happen to a burglar."

The others in the group laughed as her mother said, "I think she's trying to get out of the tour! Aren't you honey?" A red flush popped out on her cheeks. I felt so bad for her. I knew these tours weren't for everyone, she was probably bored out of her skull.

Myra moved further into the center hall area of the second floor room. The whole tour group shuffled in close to hear.

She explained that we were now above the large library hall downstairs. "This area once held an oversized, sturdy table. Twice a year it was used by the seamstress to outfit the children with new clothing. No Walmart around here in those days! She would arrive on Bella, a double-decker steamboat, at the Swift wharf on the Bon Secour River. She came bearing fabrics and patterns for the children's wardrobes. I hope y'all can find the time to walk down to the river after the tour. You can still see the old wharf pilings where boats tied up."

Pointing to an open door leading outside, Myra said, "Please peek out on this verandah. You can gaze across the grounds to the School House Creek. I understand Mr. Nik Coles spent many pleasant hours in this lovely spot enjoying the beautiful view."

I glanced around hoping the Ouija board was still here. It was!

"Any questions before we move into the bedrooms?"

I raised my hand. Myra didn't notice as she had already turned to take the group into the first bedroom.

"Did you have a question lass? I might be able to help you." It was the lady who had picked up the girl's phone speaking. Her voice had an Irish lilt, soft and rolling. I remembered her now, from breakfast at the Tin Roof this morning.

"Do you know what this is about?" I said, pointing to the game board resting on a side table.

"Yes, I do. It is a wee controversial game named Ouija. It was sold as a parlor game but soon acquired a sinister and disturbing reputation. Spiritualists believed they could call up spirits of dead people through Ouija boards. Eventually these beliefs led to it being banned in many a parlor."

I figured it had to be something like that. I remembered the girls saying they were calling up the spirit of Laurens de Graaf. Kind of spooky feeling seeing it just sitting here so innocent now. How many years ago had the girls played on it? Must be at least a hundred years ago.

"You've met the girls haven't you dear?"

How could she possibly know that? I stuttered. "...ah...sort of...I guess."

She said, "Good." Then, with a little goodbye wave she joined the group crowding into the first bedroom.

"Hey wait," I said as I followed behind her. I heard Myra explaining that the little blue coat displayed on the bed belonged to Ira, one of the Swift children. The Irish lady was nowhere to be seen.

8

MEETING MATT

The boy walking up to the big house must be Matt, Charlie thought. His thin arms, poking out of his oversized tee shirt, were tanned a nutty brown. Dusty toes in black flip flops peeked out from frayed and worn-through-at-the-knees jeans. He looked expectantly at Charlie and grinned. Charlie smiled back, happy to have a buddy to run around with.

When introductions were over and after a few moments of awkwardness, Grauntie Nora suggested the boys join the next group waiting on the front porch.

Matt hesitated before saying, "Ah....nice of you to offer, but I'd like to show Charlie around. I've been here a few times and I can give him an outside tour of the place if that's all right with you ma'am."

Nora could hardly stifle a laugh, before she said, "Hmm...I hadn't thought of that. A grounds tour? Might be a suggestion for Myra, something to add to the itinerary."

"Good idea Grauntie. I'll let you know how he does. Come on, let's go," Charlie quickly piped in, before pulling Matt down the porch steps.

They ran around the side of the house. The stones forming the path were worn down and rocked unevenly as the boys raced across them.

Matt stopped by a small, white building with a criss-cross lattice-work screen concealing the entry door. "What do you think this was used for?"

Charlie peeked his head inside. "Looks like some kind of game. Like a bean bag toss only with gigantic beanbags."

"Nope, guess again."

"Some place to store vegetables or something?" Charlie went further into the small building. A rough plank structure, about the height of a chair seat with four rather large holes cut in the surface, took up over half the floor space. "And then those pieces of wood are like lids to cover the stuff up from animals getting in?"

Charlie bent over to peer into the openings. He couldn't see far down into the darkness, but the holes seemed to go pretty deep. "Reminds me of the recycling bins at school. The two bigger ones for paper and glass and the other two smaller ones for plastic and food waste. Is that right Matt?"

"Well now, it is sort of recycling system. A real old one though. Probably even before they had plastic," Matt said.

As Charlie closely inspected the little room, he heard someone outside say, "My grannie had one of those on the farm, only it was a single seater. I hear this one has four seats!"

Someone else laughed and replied, "No privacy for someone needing to do their business for sure."

Do their business? It slowly dawned on him what he was sticking his face into. He let out a yelp before chasing after the figure of the fleeing Matt.

Matt tripped and stumbled. Charlie fell over him. Between breaths, Charlie said, "Matt, how could you?"

"Sorry buddy, but I couldn't resist. Isn't that just the grossest thing? Picture sharing would you?"

"No, I don't want to picture that!" Charlie rolled into a ball he was laughing so hard. "I can't believe you let me stick my head down those holes. I owe you one." Charlie was sure Matt was going to be fun to hang around with.

"Hey let's walk over to the oyster shell mounds on the river," Matt said.

"What are those?"

"Come on I'll show you."

Matt grabbed the fishing poles he'd left by the front gate and took Charlie to the banks of the river.

"Matt, did pirates ever come here?"

"Not sure."

"Do you think there is any pirate treasure around here?"

"Not sure about that either. Pa thinks so. He's always hoping to strike it rich. Guess he figures finding some gold doubloons is a good way. He usually gets talking about it when he's had a few drinks or a bad day at fishing."

"Hey, want to take the Captain Jack Pirate Adventure Cruise together?"

"Sounds good. I've never been on it," Matt said. "So Charlie, why couldn't the pirate play cards?"

"Hmm, because he was sitting on the deck?"

Jabbing him in the side, Matt said, "That's right! Let's get fishing."

Skeletons of once bustling wharves littered the river shoreline. Tall wooden pilings lashed together with rope, stood isolated from the gray boards of abandoned piers fanning down toward their watery grave.

Mounds of oyster half shells lay discarded on the river's edge. Pulled from their watery beds and spilt open by shuckers. Their inner, mucus-like life taken out. The shells, with their rough protective outer surfaces and smooth nurturing interior surfaces, tossed aside to bleach to a pale gray in the southern sun.

The river rippled, reflecting the white clouds hanging above in the blue sky. Gulls called and fussed over the boys. Pelicans glided by, scouting for food.

The boys settled in to some quiet fishing time on the banks of the Bon Secour. Little did they know what the river had in store for them.

9

LILLIA

I never did see the Irish lady again that day. I don't know how she got out of that bedroom without me seeing her. But more important, how did she know about last night and the Swift sisters?

After the house closed for the day, Myra told me I was welcome to wander wherever I wanted. So I decided to explore while Myra and Grauntie enjoyed sweet tea on the verandah.

The room with the antiques seemed like it might be interesting so it was the first place I headed. And it sure was a good choice, because as soon as I unhooked the velvet cord draped across the door and stepped inside, things flew at me.

Pieces of paper, yellowed with time, and colorful embroidered squares, like little flying carpets, floated past. The small cover of a Chinese porcelain jar rose and started a slow twirl. Glass paneled doors in the front of a highly polished wood cabinet swung open, revealing shiny silver bowls in which oddly colored soups steamed.

I heard a throat clearing sound. Seated by a desk, inlaid with golden, swirling designs, sat a man dressed in strange clothing. His shirt had ruffles at the neck and cuffs. His pants came to just below his knees. White stockings covered the calves of his legs. His shoes were the oddest things, black with big, shiny, metal buckles.

His back was to me, but I could tell by the tilt of his head that he was studying something on the desktop. He reached across to a small bottle. I saw a long, white feather in his hand. He dipped the end into the bottle and returned to writing.

He was talking with someone. The voices wavered in and out. The words were coming to me in a different language but my mind understood them.

A white rose in a narrow vase appeared on a small table near the door. Then a woman in a long, full-skirted, ivory dress crossed in front of me. She bent to breath in the floral sweetness. Her hair, pinned with glittering combs, gathered in luscious loops piled high atop her head. "Is it true that the cargo never made it my love?"

"I'm afraid so. Appears that our Anne Dieu-li-Veut secured France's gold from those thieving Spaniards. However, my dear, I am sad to say I received word that rapscallion pirates brutally attacked her ship. All may be lost. I am entering it in my journal as such. I do wish her and her family, along with the crew, Godspeed."

I listened carefully. A Frenchman? Anne worked for him?

"So her family was lost as well?" the woman asked as she glided by me and passed on through an outside wall. I watched her float up to a yard statue and melt into the form of a cherub raising a trumpet.

Beyond, on the open lawn, a group of artists were positioned behind easels. They sat expressing themselves with art, while here I stood, history moving around me. These pieces, particles, and energies from the past were taking form in my imagining.

I saw one of the painters wave and flash a big smile… the Irish lady. What?

I jumped when the Frenchman pounded his fist on the secretary. "Those blasted pirate thieves. How dare they steal from us? Perhaps killing a young boy in the raid? Dastardly scum!"

I needed to leave before one of my imaginings breaks something and I get blamed for it. Slamming fists on fancy French desks from the another century was not a good idea.

I left the room, hooking the cord back up. The space quietly returned to what it was, a showcase for rare and precious antiques.

Except that the flower in the vase on the small table remained. And next to it lay a note with my name on it.

Delicately I reached across the velvet cord and plucked the folded paper up. It read…

The sad tale was begun,
Long ago and faraway,
When a Pirate Queen lost her son,
One awful sorrowful day.

She has watched his burial site,
For over three hundred years.
Many the man who has fled in fright,
When the Pirate Queen appears.

10

SEEING GHOSTS

"So there you are. Did you explore the house a little more?" Grauntie asked, thinking Lillia was a looking frazzled.

Lillia nodded. "Yes, and Myra, thank you so much for letting me poke around. I love old places."

Myra took a sip of her iced tea and patted her lips with a napkin before saying, "That's so good to hear. We love to show the house to appreciative guests like you. When did you get such an interest in historical buildings?"

"I'm not sure. I like to imagine the people that lived in them. The things that happened. It's just sort of fun for me."

"Lillia doesn't like to say much about her special abilities…" Nora said. Lillia shot her a please-don't-say-anymore look which Nora smoothly deflected by continuing her sentence, "…which are quite something. She seems to absorb pieces of actions, words, feelings, energies from the past. Then, like those artists on the lawn interpret the essence of what they observe by putting it in a painting, Lillia can take what she feels and create an imagining from a past moment in time."

Myra said, "Oh, I know what you mean! Sometimes when I'm in the house by myself I stand and let the family whisper to me. If I close my eyes I can picture them and almost feel them passing by me. Like they are here with me, or I am back in history with them. Time loses meaning."

Nora said," Sounds like a similar sort of extra sensory thing. Lillia's subconscious mind can imagine another level of time and place with energies and pieces from the past."

Myra laid her hand over her heart. "Oh, I would love to be able to do that." She hesitated. "This may sound silly to y'all, but sometimes, when I'm doing that pretend thing with my eyes closed...I peek."

Lillia smiled and said, "And..."

"I see fleeting glimpses of them. Ghostly images at the edge of my vision."

"Like floaters?" Nora asked.

Myra nodded vigorously. "Exactly!"

Lillia said," What are floaters?"

Myra laughed, reaching to pat Lillia's hand. "You are too young to know about floaters. Old people like us have them."

"They are little cloud-like pieces inside the eyeball. Once in a while, they drift across your vision. But if you try to really check them out, they slide away," Nora said. "You are aware of them, but can't study them because they just float away."

"Hmm...," Lillia said.

"Well, enough of all this talk. Time to get headed home for this old gal. See y'all tomorrow," Myra said, pushing herself off the wicker chair.

"Thanks for the tea and the visit. Would you mind dropping Matt back at Tin Roof, please? I told Cecelia he'd be home in time for dinner."

"Sure, be happy to. Where are the boys?"

"Lillia, would you see if you can find them?"

Lillia leaned out over the porch railing and yelled, "Matt... Charlie...time to go."

"Oh good grief," Nora said with a smile, "I could have done that!"

"Well it did the trick. There they are," Myra said, pointing down the road to the wharf.

"Someone call?" Charlie shouted.

LILLIA

I don't like Grauntie talking about my imaginings with other people. Mostly I don't want to have a special ability as she puts it. Sometimes people make fun of me for it, or it confuses them and they leave me. I'm not a detective following clues, or a scientist discovering another planet, I want to be just Lillia, a twelve-year-old girl from Kansas.

I've learned that it is usually best to not even bring it up with my friends and for sure not with Mom. When my imagining ability helped solve the mystery of Miss Margaret's missing family in Kentucky, I made it seem that serendipity did it, not me. And looking back, I know fate and luck did have a big part in it.

Tonight I had a hard time staying awake until Grauntie and Charlie went to sleep. I was excited to go back and visit Miriam, Eleanor, Emily and Nell. Miriam said they had watched for me because of the note. And now I had the note from the antique room about the Pirate Queen losing her son. Where is this burial site? Maybe they have some ideas. I have to see them again.

Stepping out into the back hall, I pulled the apartment door closed behind me. I held the knob turned open until the little clicky thing slipped quietly into place. Whew, made it out without waking Grandma or Charlie.

Just enough moonlight entered through the back windows to show me the three steps up to the master bedroom. At least I could go this back way and not up the full staircase where that girl had tripped today.

I made my way around the big four poster bed. A reflection moved in the mirror of the tall wooden armoire. A woman straightening her black dress. This place was so cool...stuff like that all over. Love it! I gave her a little smile. Reaching for a black bonnet hanging from the bedpost, she smiled back at me before fading away.

The large center upstairs hall room looked different now. A big table dominated the space. Soft blue fabric lay in ripples across one corner of the table, with a drift of shimmery buttons floating on top of the flow. A thick, strong, brown wool stood in a folded stack on the far end. In-between lay delicate paper pattern pieces, resting on a cotton fabric sprinkled with red and yellow flowers.

Thin, gauzy, white material, piled in fluffy mounds, gathered around the figure of a young woman sitting on a stool. She worked intently, head bent over, one hand gently gathering the softness while her other hand pushed a needle and thread through it. In and out. In and out.

I stood mesmerized, watching. The seamstress seemed not to notice me.

The girls were not here. I whispered, "Miriam, I'm here. It's Lillia. The girl who visited you last night."

Nothing.

It had been after the twelfth strike of the clock last night when I found them. I couldn't remember hearing the chimes tonight. Maybe I was too early? Or they were waiting for me outside? I walked over to a window and peered out to the front yard.

I caught a glimpse of lights far away, down toward where the river must be. On the tour I'd heard Myra explain that a road used to go from the big house to the pier. The Swift family could watch the double-decker steamships arriving at the wharf. Was that the direction I was looking? Could they be down there? Hard to tell with the overgrown trees half blocking the view.

Since I was up anyway, I decided to go and check it out.

Footsteps sounded behind me. Hooray, they were here.

12

THE NIGHT WATCHMAN

"Hey Lil, what are you doing up here?"

"Don't sneak up on me like that!"

"Sorry, but I woke up and you weren't on the couch," Charlie said in his don't-yell-at-me voice.

Lillia said, "I couldn't sleep so I was exploring the house."

"In the dark?"

"Yes, in the dark! My eyes get used to it and I do fine. Now go back to bed," Lillia said.

Charlie said, "No, I want to stay up. I can't sleep either. Can we go outside? This house gives me the creeps."

"Oh all right. Hey, I thought I saw some lights in the direction of that old abandoned wharf. Was going to head down there and check it out. Guess you can come along, but you've got to promise to behave and not bounce around all over."

"I will."

"There might be ghosts of the girls who lived here. So you can't get all scared."

Charlie's eyes lit up. "Or pirate ghosts?"

"Is that all you can think of? No. No pirates. Dad was kidding when he told you those stories."

"He was not. How would you know anyway? This is just the kind of place pirates would hide. Dad said so. He knows a bunch about them. Like how they were scary, bad guys."

"Not always, Charlie. Some of those so-called pirates did things for their governments, technically they had permission."

"You think I'm stupid don't you?" Charlie just shook his head. "Who would believe something like that?"

"I don't care if you believe it or not."

"Well I don't believe you," Charlie said.

"Fine! Whatever. Google the word privateers and you'll see for yourself smarty. So want to go down to the wharf or are you too scared?"

Charlie stomped down the stairs ahead of Lillia. Scared? I'll show her I can handle the dark.

The cacophony of buzzing, clicking and chirping hit Lillia and Charlie as soon as they left the house. After a few moments, it settled into a typical evening symphony of insects among the trees and flowers.

Lillia screamed as a black flapping something, with

jerky flying movements, darted towards them, before quickly veering away.

Charlie jumped. "Don't scream like that. It was only a bat."

"I didn't scream!"

"Yes, you did!"

"Don't know why you're so frightened by spiders and snakes and stuff like that," Charlie said.

"It's just when they come out suddenly. When they catch me by surprise. Besides you're afraid of the dark so look who's talking."

"Forget about it. I'm going back to the house. You can go by yourself."

"Fine."

"Fine with me too. Bye."

"Bye."

Lillia turned to head further down the path. Charlie changed his mind and followed behind her.

Lillia spun around quickly and shouted, "Boo!"

Charlie let out a loud yell.

A voice called out, "Who's there?"

Lillia held her finger up to her closed lips to quiet Charlie.

Next thing they knew, a bright light was turned on and aimed right at them. Both Lillia and Charlie raised their hands to shield their eyes.

"What you kids doing out here? You aren't supposed to be wandering around here this time of night."

Charlie piped up, "We saw some strange lights down this way. Down near the water. We're staying in the big house and figured we'd better check them out."

"You did now did you?" said the man behind the flashlight.

"And why are you out here in the dark?" Charlie asked, bold as you please.

"I'm paid to be out here."

With a biggest humph sound he could muster Charlie said, "Who would pay someone to be out walking around at night? That's crazy."

"Guess the owners of the seafood processing plant back there are crazy then. I'll be sure to let them know some kid I met last night said that."

Lillia punched Charlie in the arm. "He's a night watchman. Sorry sir, but we didn't know this was part of the fish plant property. We were following this old overgrown drive down to the water's edge."

"It's not on their property actually. But I can tell you there's nothing going on tonight. For once."

"Well thank you, but we'll walk down and see for ourselves. Now if you'll please excuse us," Charlie said.

"You will now will you? What if I said I don't think you should?"

"Guess I'd have to politely disagree," Charlie said, without missing a beat.

"Ha ha," the man said as he slapped his chest. "If you two aren't the darndest thing I've run into out here."

Lillia asked, "You mean you run into things wandering around a lot this time of night?"

"I do every once in a while. Sometimes I catch young teenagers out here messing around by the ruins of Meme's Cafe. Dangerous for them. The place could fall in on top of them," he said, as he turned the flashlight to shine up and cast big shadows over his face. Shadows that moved eerily as he leaned in and murmured, "But the strangest things I come upon, are happening after midnight by the old dock area."

"Like what?" Charlie said with a big gulp.

"If I tell you, I'll have to kill you," he said without expression. His eyes were black holes shaded from the light beam.

13

LILLIA

I couldn't breathe. What had I gotten us into?

"Oh come on now, just kidding!"

Charlie cracked up. "Good one. You had us hooked and reeled in!"

I was less amused.

The man said," Well, you two go on and check it out. But be careful where you're walking. I don't need to pull anyone out of the river tonight." He reached into his pant pocket and pulled out a smaller flashlight. "Here you take this. It's my spare. Leave it on the front bench tomorrow if I'm not around. My place is the old one end of this road, by the tall pilings."

"Thanks. Come on Lillia, let's head on down. Hey mister, do you know if any pirates came to this place?"

"Well now young man, I surely do. I'm kind of a

history buff about this Bon Secour River area. Why right where you two are headed there's been all sorts of boats pulled up. Bon Secour means safe harbor in French, and that it has been for hundreds of years. During the Civil Wars, them darn Yankees would land right here and we Southerners had to give them salt from our salt mines. Salt was precious as gold to them during those times. And French trappers and fishermen came up this river to explore. Many eventually settled here. They even built a resort."

Charlie said, "But pirates, were there pirates?"

"Pirates most certainly roamed these parts."

I wasn't sure about this guy. He seemed innocent enough. Better ask Myra about him, though.

A big part of me wanted to ask him if he'd ever heard of any female pirates, but instead, I said, "Thank you for the offer of the light, but we should be getting back."

"Take the flashlight with you. I know the drill. Don't talk to strangers. You ask that Miss Myra about me. She'll let you know I'm a good guy. Good night now and sorry if I scared you."

"Hey, thanks mister. Could you maybe tell me more about the pirates some time? And if there is buried treasure here?"

"Treasure like gold and gems?"

Charlie nodded.

"I've heard stories. A few gold doubloons have been found over the years. Some folks figure that buried treasure was lifted by tides or storm waters and broke apart. Guess it could be true."

Charlie turned to give me the eye. "So there might be treasure? Did you hear that Lillia? Hey mister, what's a pirate's favorite letter?"

The man tapped the side of his head and scrunched up his face. "A?"

"Nope."

More sharply, this time, I said, "Come on, leave him alone now. Good night, sir."

With a big goofy grin, the man said, "Is it arrrr?"

"That's right...you got it!" Charlie gave a thumbs up. "Good night, mister. My name is Charlie."

"Charlie. A good name. I'm Pierre Gavin, but folks call me Pete. Pleasure to meet you."

The man stood watching as we walked away. Then, when we almost out of earshot, he called out, "Oh, and Charlie..."

Charlie stopped and peered back over his shoulder.

"I'll bet money that there is treasure here."

Charlie grinned and gave him two thumbs up.

We walked back to the big house without talking.

The row of iron hitching posts greeting us as we arrived back at the house. Patting the horse head on top of each one as he paraded by, Charlie said, "So see, I wasn't being a stupid kid thinking there might be treasure buried here."

With a smirk I said, "Think what you want." I knew

that I had to focus on finding a site someone was actually watching. Not a site where some old pirates had maybe buried some kind of treasure. Probably never happened anyway. Except on Dora the Explorer television shows.

14

SEA LIFE

The next morning Lillia and Charlie were waiting in the drive when Cecelia and Matt pulled up, dust rising and swirling behind the old truck she drove.

"Morning kiddies. What a beautiful day the Lord gave us! Near on perfect for lads and lassie to cruise out to the deep blue sea," Cecelia called out her open window as she slid to a stop at the edge of the road.

"Thought we were just going out to Mobile Bay?" Lillia asked.

"Yes, you are matey. I'm just setting up the pirate thing a bit."

"Well then, shiver me timbers," Lillia said, "...and yo ho ho...and...that's about all I know!"

Cecelia let out a loud laugh. "Well y'all will be learning some more pirate talk soon, because Captain Jack's cruise is a dandy. He's a whole pile of fun!"

Matt got out to let Lillia sit inside the cab with Cecelia. He jumped up on the rear bumper and hopped into the bed of the red pickup. Charlie quickly joined Matt. Mom and Dad would not be happy seeing this he thought. No seat belt. Not even a seat!

"Hey is that Captain Jack like Jack Sparrow in Pirates of the Caribbean?" Lillia asked Cecelia.

"Lordy girl I don't know about that. This gal don't get to many movies. But I will admit, he cuts a rather dashing figure if I do say so myself." Matt and Charlie started snickering and giggling, loud enough for Cecelia to hear them. "And don't you youngin's laugh. I cut a pretty dashing figure myself at one time!"

Matt said," Sorry Grannie. It's just so weird hearing you talk about a guy being dashing. That means good right?"

"It surely does. Lillia did you bring sunscreen? You will be out in the weather for over four hours so you best be protected."

Lillia fumbled through the bag Grauntie had packed. Water bottles, a bag of carrot sticks, three granola bars, money for the tickets and there, at the bottom, the sunscreen. "Got it."

They drove through a thin forest before taking a right on the river road. The sunlight made the Bon Secour River glisten. A motor boat passed, leaving behind a sparkling wake.

Charlie watched a gull dive down into the water. "Wow look at that!"

"Found himself a little food churned up by the boat's motor," Matt said. "Watch, there goes another."

A pair of kayakers paddled along the far shore. Across the river, small private piers, weathered and gray, jutted out over the water.

The river road passed by some ramshackle buildings with fading signs painted on their walls. The road surface was made of discarded oyster shells, bleached white in the sun and crushed into small rough pieces.

Soon they entered the wharf's parking lot. Shrimp boats, with their outriggers standing tall, held out shrimp nets that draped elegantly into the water. Names proudly painted on their hulls...Lady Kris, Captain Ben, Michele Dawn.

Cecelia pulled in and parked near the entrance to Tommy's where a red and white sign reading, 'If it swims...We've got it!' had welcomed shoppers for generations.

Inside Tommy's Seafood Market, smells of the ocean and the life taken from it permeated the painted wooden walls, scuffed floorboards, and simple cabinets.

"Morning boys," Cecelia said as she walked the length of the room eyeing the tubs holding seafood. Limp legged shrimp bodies piled on top of one other. Fish lay side by side on icy beds. Oyster shells, waiting to be opened, mounded on a sideboard.

A tall man in a gray rubber apron, with smatterings of

blood and fish guts on it, called out, "Hey Miss C how's it going? What is the Tin Roof going to be needing today?"

"Morning Chuck. Give me eight pounds of the royal red and six of the large," Cecelia said, without taking her eyes off the display as she walked along. "Nine filets of snapper, fifteen mahi-mahis and three pounds of amberjack."

"That new grilled oyster recipe working out good for you?"

"Sure is. I'll be needing fourteen dozen oyster too. Thanks, Chuck," she said glancing up with a smile. "How's the missus? Heard she got her cast off."

"She did. In a walking boot still, but doing better without the crutches," he answered.

A man with gray hair poking out the bottom of his greasy hat, and wearing a stained green t-shirt reading Mardi Gras in purple and gold letters, pointed his dirty calloused finger at Matt and said, "Well if it ain't old Hank's son. What's your name boy?"

Matt ducked his head and mumbled his name.

"Say again boy. And look up. I'm talkin' at you."

Matt shook his head and ran out of the shop. Charlie dashed after him, but not before shooting the old man a dirty look.

Cecelia said, "Leave the boy alone. You got some beef with his pa, you take it to him."

"You bet I got a beef with Hank. He owes me near two hundred bucks."

Cecelia shrugged, before turning her back to him and returning to her seafood buying. "No problem of mine."

From behind the counter, Chuck added, "Shut your mouth old man. There's young ones and ladies here. Why don't you go out back and see if they've weighed in your catch?"

The man mumbled something under his breath. He left through the passageway to the back of the shop where the boats pulled up to unload.

"Anything else for you Miss C?"

"No thanks that should do it. Who was that guy?"

"Never mind him, just an old timer here. Hank's been borrowing money again and not showing up to work when the guys need another deckhand. No cause to pick on the kid though."

Cecelia grit her teeth. It was never going to end. That man couldn't work more than a few days in a row. He was supposed to join his son today. Have some father and son time taking the cruise. Probably best he didn't show up. Stella, my dear departed daughter, you want me to help Matt know his pa, but Lordy he makes it hard.

15

LILLIA

I looked out through the smudged windows of Tommy's. Life on the river. How simple and real this place was. No fancy lighting or classical music. These boats just doing their job. The men taking them out day after day. Working to bring their catch back in and earn money to live on.

Some of this seafood would go up the road to the Tin Roof for the local people to eat. Some flown away to other cities. Tonight a dressed up couple in Chicago might be eating two of those fresh snapper in a restaurant on Michigan Avenue. A few of those jumbo shrimp could hop a flight to Kansas where Mom and Dad might enjoy them. I liked the picture of them going out to together. They seemed to be arguing more and more every day instead of how it used to be.

I overheard another man near me. "Man's right to be

mad with that Hank. He's skating on pretty thin ice around here. He messes with one of us, he messes with all of us."

Poor Matt, seems like his dad is not too well liked in here. I was glad Charlie had walked out with him. Must be embarrassing for Matt.

"Okay then, let's head out to see if old captain Jack is ready to set sail," Cecelia said. "Pack my order up Chuck and I'll be back shortly."

"Your car right outside?" Chuck asked. "Open up the trunk and we'll put it in your coolers."

"Thanks."

A large, pink convertible drove by and pulled in next to Cecelia's pickup truck. What a crew! Laughing, chatting, and hanging on to their wide brimmed, straw hats until the car stopped. The woman driving wore a loud tropical print shirt and white rimmed sunglasses. Next to her sat a woman with the brightest red lipstick I'd ever seen, and hot pink polka dots on her blouse. The rear seat passenger sprawled across the seat, the lime green of her dress repeated in plastic bangle bracelets and earrings.

I heard Charlie whisper to Matt," Wow they are old."

Matt nodded his agreement. "Their skin is so wrinkly."

I smiled when I saw that one was the little Irish lady!

Cecelia said, "Well bless my heart if they don't look like just the happiest bunch of gals. Hey ladies," she called, "y'all come to sail with Captain Jack?"

"We surely are. Every year we take the Captain Jack Pirate Adventure Cruise together. Then buy some fresh shrimp from Tommy's to celebrate life and friendship," the driver said.

Oh good! They were going on the cruise with us.

Next to them was a van with a family of young children spilling out. The mother climbed out slowly, running her fingers through her hair and giving her neck a little rub. I noticed a cute boy opening the rear door to pull out a baby stroller. Twin girls with hair pulled up into pigtails, round chubby cheeks, excited eyes, and big smiles were already running around. The dad had wandered over to the edge of the river to check out the boats tied in the harbor.

"Ken, watch her!" the mom shouted, as one of the girls toddled out into the parking lot.

The dad leaped into action and snagged the little one up, tossing her a few inches and catching her as he did a full spin around. Dad always did that with me when I was little. When did he stop? Or did I stop wanting him to? Did I decide it might look silly to other people?

Loud music started up and all of our heads turned to find the source.

It came from a very old looking ship flying the Jolly Roger, a black skull and crossbones flag. A man dressed in a white shirt, with long pants tucked into leather boots, and dark hair trailing out from under a three-corner hat, gave a big wave.

The twins started dancing, wiggling their entire bodies to the music. The three women threw back their heads and swung their arms to the rhythm as they sang, "Yo ho a pirate's life for me'."

"Let the pirate shenanigans begin right now!" Cecelia sang out as she did a small jig.

"Blimey and shiver me timbers if there isn't a bunch of landlubbers ready to board me mighty ship!"

"That has to be Captain Jack," Charlie said, practically jumping up and down.

Jack stood with shoulders thrown back, gold earring shining, and a hand on his cutlass. "Give me a cheer lads and lassies."

Charlie, the twins, and the three old ladies let out a whoop.

Then with a deep bow, he took off his hat and swept it dramatically across his chest. "And I see my three pirate queens are back. Welcome me sweet vixens."

The women giggled and waved.

"And I'll be an ole sea dog if it ain't Miss Cecelia! Will ye be boarding my fine sailing vessel this bright and sunny day?"

She put her hands on her broad hips and looked up at Captain Jack. "Pshaw, you old scallywag. I've got too much work to do. But my grandson and his friends will listen to your tall tales."

"Feisty wrench now, ain't ye? Your loss my sweet."

With a big laugh, Cecelia said, "Great to see you again too Jack. Take care of the kids and safe travels."

"Aye aye. All hands hoay!"

The three women started up the gangplank and Captain Jack took each one's hand to help her over the edge. Matt and Charlie boarded.

Next, the father holding the hands of his twin daughters walked up the wobbly plank. The mom came by pushing the stroller, struggling to carry her purse, camera and diaper bag.

Her son reached to take the bag just as I said, "Can I help you push the stroller?"

She nodded wearily with grateful eyes. "That would be nice. Thank you."

At the edge of the plank, Jack bent and lifted the front end of the stroller up, dipping the baby back and making her giggle and kick her little legs.

When everyone was settled on board, Jack said, "Welcome, all ye who enter here. We set sail for the high seas of the mighty Gulf of Mexico where ruthless bands of buccaneers roamed."

As we pulled away from the dock, I heard Cecelia call out, "Be good y'all and listen to Captain Jack."

16

CAPTAIN JACK'S CRUISE

The Captain Jack Pirate Adventure Cruise was underway.

From their perches on old pilings, brown pelicans watched as the ship passed. Jack pointed out this ancient creature with its awkward appearance. He explained that it had been depicted in art over hundreds of years as a mother very attentive to her young. Now and then one would swoop away, gracefully, lightly, effortlessly. With lift off, their broad wings spread, appearing as if they weighed next to nothing.

Once clear of the river and out into Bon Secour Bay, Captain Jack set the ship at cruising speed. He passed out Pirate Booty Bags to everyone. The treat bags held felt pirate hats, red nylon sashes, a plastic cutlass, a list of favorite pirate words, gold foil coins, and a treasure map.

The three women promptly took off their sun hats and

put on the pirate hats, snapping the elastic string under their chins. The twins went for the shiny foil coins and soon discovered the chocolate inside.

Lillia fashioned the red scarf as a tie around her hip and inserted the cutlass. She saw the twins were getting covered in chocolate. The mom tossed Lillia some wipes and the chase was on. The twins giggled and ducked away but Lillia weaved in and out, cornered them, and wiped their faces and hands off.

Their brother was reading from the list of pirate words. As Lillia went by she leaned in and said, "What's a pirate's favorite letter?"

"Arrrr?"

"Yep! Hi my name's Lillia."

"I'm Tod. Wait..." he ran his finger down the list and added, "...ahoy mate."

Lillia grinned.

Captain Jack understood that all young boys and girls want to be pirates. They want to picture themselves free and unafraid, strong and cunning, living life without rules. He had met grown men who had never gotten over wanting to be pirates.

Matt and Charlie were pouring over their treasure maps. Charlie said, "It's a real map. Here's the river and Tommy's and the big house. I can see where the river goes further inland. This part says we should explore life and discover our own treasure."

Matt said, "Don't you get it? The map is made up for

BRENDA FELBER

tourists. It means like find your treasure in life, the things you value. Ahh, like find..."

"...a favorite fishing hole?" Charlie asked.

"Something like that."

"But we could still use the map to explore with. Right?"

"Guess so," Matt mumbled.

"And listen...here's a poem printed on the map. 'Many hear the tales told, and feel the powerful lure, of finding the chests of gold, on the banks of the Bon Secour.' Cool!"

"Well then Charlie, let's find that chest when we get back," Matt said, gazing out over the water. "We'll find our treasure."

They cruised across Mobile Bay. Oil derricks rose from the water. Ferry boats loaded with cars and passengers passed by them.

Dipping south, Captain Jack pointed out Fort Morgan, a Civil War fort open for tours, at the tip of the land to the left.

Then he shouted, "Dolphins! Starboard side."

Everyone's attention was drawn to the dolphins. Beautiful, streamlined creatures, riding the wake. Rolling and leaping from the surface up into the air. They followed the ship, performing their antics, as the ship maneuvered toward an island ahead.

Captain Jack pointed it out, saying, "There's Dauphin Island. Dauphin means dolphin in French."

He told the story of explorers finding mounds of human bones when they arrived and naming it Massacre

Island before they knew the bones were part of Indian burial mounds.

Charlie piped up, "So Captain Jack, were there ever pirates on this island?"

"Scoundrels hid their ships behind it. They watched and waited for Spanish galleons returning from South America laden with gold. Then surprise! Out they raced to rob them."

Tod said, "I heard about a lost city of gold in South America. Was that story real?"

"Well now laddie, many a man died in South America searching for the place called El Dorado. But I'll tell ye a truth. It never existed."

He spoke lower and everyone leaned in to listen. "The Spanish searched and searched for El Dorado, but turns out it wasn't a place or a city at all. It was a man. The Muisca people used gold dust in a ceremony to honor their leaders. They didn't value gold for wealth like the Europeans did. But the myth grew."

Captain Jack paused, glancing toward the island we were passing. "So you see my buccaneers, treasure means one thing to those seeking it and another to those who have it."

What he had been trying to say, may have been lost on some, but the mom hugged her baby a little tighter and the three old ladies patted each other's hands and leaned in together.

Charlie, however, didn't miss a beat. "But the pirates

did steal the gold when the Spanish guys sailed back with it?"

"Yes, young Charles they did."

Wide-eyed, Charlie checked out the island. "Did they ever go up into the Bon Secour Bay to bury it?"

"Aye laddie, they did."

17

LILLIA

I saw Captain Jack let Charlie and Matt steer the ship. Charlie would have fun dreams tonight, not those weird ones he has sometimes. Matt seemed very focused and interested in what Jack was telling him. I could tell he was asking lots of questions.

The sky had been clouding over. Seemed like the trip back to Bon Secour would be a little cooler.

The twins were fast asleep. Their mother looked ready to nod off as well. Tod and his dad watched the distant shore-line go by. I had found out they were staying near the big house. Tod said maybe they'd come by for a tour. I hoped so.

I walked toward the prow and proclaimed, "I'm the queen of the world." I threw my arms out wide.

"Yes, you are."

I spun around to see the Irish lady standing next to me.

She ducked just in time to miss my arm hitting her upside the head. "Oops so sorry!"

"I shouldn't have startled you like that," she said, taking off her pirate hat before the wind did it for her.

"My bad. Just pretending to be in the Titanic movie. Can I ask you something?"

"Yes, Lillia?"

"How'd you know my name? And how did you know that I met the Swift sisters?"

"I'm like Emily," she said.

"Emily Swift?"

"No, Emily from Land Between the Lakes in Kentucky. The spirit guide who helped you during your time there."

I remembered that Emily very well. The message she gave me, saying I could help someone in Bon Secour. She appeared to other people but then didn't show up on Zoe's photo. And she had done that weird thing on the Living Farm where she appeared inside my imagining. Could this sweet little old lady really be like that?

Hmm…maybe I should see what she is capable of. "When you were painting with the artists out on the lawn yesterday, did you see me in the window?"

"Yes, I did. I even added the man seated at the desk to my painting." She giggled. "I was feeling a wee bit ambitious."

She saw that imagined man? Then she must be like Emily, a spirit guide.

"Lillia dear, I'm here to help you. But you are the imagineer. There are very few imagineers in the world. And of those, only the rare one who can do what you can. You are young in this path. You will grow."

"Well I'll take any help I can get right now. With all this pirate talk you'd think I'd get a clue where to look for the pirate lady I'm supposed to help."

"What more have you learned about her?" she asked me.

"Her name is Anne. Her husband Laurens wants her to quit watching whatever she's watching. That day you saw me in the antique room, I heard a conversation about Anne, between the guy you saw and a lady in the room. Oh, and another verse was left for me. This makes three of those."

She winked and said, "So you've been getting the verses? Good, I hoped so. I tried to get them to you sooner." She shrugged. "Guess the powers that be figure I'm getting a little full of it! I say, if you can't dazzle them with brilliance, baffle them with blarney."

I burst out laughing. What a character she was!

"And now I see we're almost back so I'll be saying my goodbye to you. Oh, and my name is Mairead, the Irish form of Margaret."

What? Mairead? Margaret? My mind raced. What is going on here?

"By your expression, I can see you remember the name. I know what you are thinking, and it's true. My name is like Margaret from Kentucky. Oh and one thing more dear, before you go doing anything so drastic like when you took a little boat across a big lake in a storm to help Margaret, there's something I feel you should know."

She went on to tell me that another imagineer, many decades ago, had tried to reach out to Anne, and was almost killed by her. Mairead told me that with the population growing in the area, the Pirate Queen was bound to be feeling even more threatened by people.

"Well, my imagineer extraordinaire, toodles for now. Be careful."

"I will. Thank you for the information."

Our Pirate Adventure Cruise was coming to an end. I saw Cecelia waiting for us in the parking lot.

I watched as Mairead drove off with her friends. I didn't know that this would be the last time I would see her.

18

GHOST SHIPS

Matt and Charlie were excited to hear that Cecelia and Nora had arranged for a campout sleepover. They soon picked a site near Schoolhouse Creek and spent the rest of the afternoon building a teepee like structure from tree limbs, covering it with old painting tarps.

Lengthy discussions followed about the possibility of Old Boy making an appearance. They designed and set up traps that would make a noise should he decide to come out and explore.

Charlie gathered campfire wood, kindling, matches, flashlight, bedding, and food...they were ready. But it was early and way too soon to start the actual camping.

They poured over the pirate map from the Booty Bag. Could there really be pirate treasure here? Charlie was sure. Matt not so much.

"Pa always talks about it. He said where there's smoke

there's fire. Guess that means all the stories must have some truth. He thinks the Swift family, or that Creole guy before them, might know about it because they owned the land around here so long."

"Did he ever hear about them finding anything?"

"Nope. But I know about some bends in the river that don't show up on this. And a couple of channels that branch away right about here," Matt said.

Charlie grabbed a pencil from his pocket to sketch on the map.

"Hey, I'm going to return Pete's flashlight. Let's take the map with us to his house. He seemed to know something about pirates in the area," Charlie said.

Matt was less optimistic about this whole thing but figured why not.

On the front porch of the low ramshackle, pieced together house, Pete sat in his wooden, high-back rocking chair. He called out, "Welcome!" as the boys approached.

"Hi Pete," Charlie said. "Brought back the flashlight you lent us last night. This is my friend Matt."

"Matt? Is your grannie Miss Cecelia at the Tin Roof?"

"Yes, sir she is."

"Give her my best. See any more strange lights Charlie?"

Charlie laughed. "No, but I did hear more about pirates today. And you seemed to know some stuff about that. I wanted to ask you if you could help us draw on a pirate treasure map. We started but haven't gotten very much in yet."

"Let me see what you have there."

The boys perched on the railing of the porch and leaned in expectantly. Pete reached into his pocket for reading glasses and spent a moment studying the map and what the boys had drawn on it.

"This here treasure map appears to be pretty accurate with laying out Mobile Bay, Bon Secour Bay and then the river. Even this here dock."

"But it's just for kids to pretend on," Matt said.

Charlie quickly piped in, "Couldn't we use it as a starting point to put clues on if we find out any stuff?"

"It seems to map out this area pretty accurately. So they want you to figure out where the pirate treasure might be. Right?" Pete asked.

Charlie said, "I think so. Is real pirate treasure here?"

"Well, now about that. Lots of fortune hunters have come sniffing around over the years. Most left empty handed. Scared like too. Heard some of 'em swore there was someone stopping them from finding the treasure. Scaring 'em off."

"Really?" Charlie asked, all eyes and ears.

"Yep, really."

Matt said, "So the area on the map is real, big deal. Like, look at this sketch showing the pirate ship sailing in the up the river. I bet that didn't happen."

The watchman stared Matt right in the eye and said, "There you're wrong...dead wrong."

Charlie's eyes widened. "So you think pirate ships could come up all the way to here on the river?"

"Pirate ships did sail in here. So did lots of other big ships. I take a bit of pride of the models I've built of ships that sailed on this river. From French explorers to pirates, from Civil War vessels to big double decker steamers. Some time you boys will have to stop by and check out my little museum," Pete said, pushing himself up off the rocker. "Right now though I've got to get to work."

"Can you quick suggest anything we might put on the map?"

"Let me see." Pete turned the map to catch the last rays of the sun. He carefully considered the map as Charlie stared at him and Matt gazed out over the river.

After a few moments he said, "I think you should put in a channel of the river up here. You can hardly see the entrance anymore it's so grown over."

Charlie pulled the pencil out of his pocket and made a light mark where Pete's finger indicated the channel opening. "Anything else?" he asked.

"So you really believe a pirate ship came by here?" Matt asked, still keeping his eyes on the river and the sunset.

"I know it did," Pete said, returning the map to Charlie. "And I've even seen it. Late at night, when things are quiet, the ships come here again…all of them."

19

LILLIA

I had a new favorite spot, a swing hanging on chains from the ceiling of Nik's upper porch. Just perfect for watching the world go by as Grandpa used to say.

Grauntie asked me, "Did you have fun on the cruise today?"

"It was nice. A little hokey, but better once we got out on the bay and the waters opened up. The little kids sure enjoyed themselves. Oh and there was this group of three old ladies who gather to take the cruise together every year."

Grauntie laughed. "Now those are my kind of old ladies. What a wonderful world we live in! So many experiences to be had and friends with traditions like that...can't beat it."

We'd sat quietly for a few moments before Grauntie said, "Did you know that this house is surrounded by a moat? Hard to see now, but at one time it was important in protecting the house from rising tidewaters."

A moat? Protected? Like a castle? Even with statues like a castle? The Swift girls probably played princesses here once upon a time.

I thought about Mairead. So much more I needed to ask her. Are there Irish fairy godmothers?

Then suddenly Grauntie gave one of her big whistles. Youch! That broke the spell. The boys were walking across the grounds. She not only caught their attention and disturbed the birds, but was probably heard by the diners at Tin Roof!

The boys gave big sweeping waves with their arms as they headed to their camp.

Grauntie yawned and stretched her arms out. "Sweetie, if you don't mind would you check on the boys later? Take a pail of water along to douse the campfire. I'm kind of beat today. This tour guide business and being on my feet all day is hitting me harder than I expected."

"No problem. I'll be up awhile yet." In fact, I planned to stay up and wait for the clock to finish striking midnight so I could visit the girls tonight.

"Oh, and could you help me out here with the tourists day after tomorrow?"

"Be happy to. Go in and put your feet up

Night on the land near the river was alive with sounds. Haunting hoots from owls hidden deep in the Spanish moss. Dull rapid clicks from hordes of bats. The gritty whine of chirping insects.

I watched the hard edges of the statues blur as twilight shadows deepened. The row of black iron horse hitching posts was barely visible in the darkness beneath the large spreading trees. The fragrance of magnolia shrubs floated to me on the balmy air.

Then I caught a whiff of something else. Eww! The harsh smell of a burning cigarette. Where was that coming from? Maybe it was from the campfire?

Later, when I walked to the campsite to douse the fire, I heard Charlie and Matt talking inside the tent. I decided not to disturb them and just poured water on the embers and turned to head back to the big house.

But the big house was gone!

In its place stood a single story, rough-sided structure. The Creole fisherman's home. This has to be the house I'd heard about being buried inside the big house.

Curiosity pulled me along, and with small steps I walked toward the home. I saw a lantern burning in one of the windows. The blurred shape of a person moved through the rooms.

The lantern was picked up by a man who brought it out to the breezeway. In his other hand he carried a small wrapped package. Holding the lantern high, he looked out, peering carefully right and left before he stepped down the wood plank steps.

He headed toward the barn, a building that only

moments ago had been buried in weedy shrubs and tangled half dead vines. Now it was a sturdy new structure he entered and I lost sight of him. The lantern pushed thin golden light beams through the cracks in the walls and out on the packed earth.

I tiptoed closer. Not sure why I thought I should be quiet. This was an imagining...he isn't real...right? I braced myself against the barn and put my eye up to one of the thin openings.

I saw him climb up on something. His reaching fingers slipped in and out of the structure of rough posts and cross beams, searching. Then, from between a beam on the top edge of the barn wall and right under the roof slope, he pulled out a shallow wooden box. Stepping down, he opened the box's lid and placed his package inside. Closing it back up and patting the surface with his hand, he put the box back in its hiding place.

Picking up the lantern, he walked out of the barn. I froze and held my breath. He moved the lantern, swinging it back and forth, squinting out into the darkness around him.

"You here?"

I didn't move.

He lifted the lamp higher and I saw his eyes. "So there you are girl!"

My stomach muscles tensed.

"What have you been chasing all day? One of the local coons again I bet."

A small hound came bouncing right by me with her tail wagging.

"One of these times a big ole gator gonna snap you up." The dog was full of herself, leaping up against the man's leg, spinning in circles as he tried to grab her. They played a minute more before the man started back to the house.

"Come on now girl. Kept your dinner waiting for you."

The dog stopped to sniff the ground, her nose sliding back and forth across it and toward me.

In a more commanding the voice, the man said, "Come." She dropped my trail and bounded up the steps and into the house ahead of the man. The door shut behind them and I was left standing in the weeds surrounding the old tilting barn under a starry sky.

I sucked in a big breath of air...then closed my eyes and let it out in a whoosh. What was hidden in the barn? And could that dog actually smell me in my imagining?

20

DARK PLACES

I n the tent, with lights out, Charlie focused on the images behind his closed eyes. He tried picturing the photos in Grauntie's digital frame passing by. Happy smiling Lillia. Change. Grand Canyon. Change. Dad cutting grass. Change. Grauntie riding horse. Change.

Night in the forest. Darkness was coming.

Breathe Charlie.

Mom riding a bike. Change. Houseboat on a lake. Change.

Darkness mangled and mashed the grasses outside the tent before it crawled in, stood up and walked around his bed.

Grandpa waving from the porch. Change.

The forest in the distance. Strange.

Faraway.

The darkness would take him and drag him to the forest. The trees would bend down and...

"Matt?"

...squeeze his chest.

"Matt, are you awake?"

Darkness paused...

"Matt, wake up."

"What's up Charlie?"

"Nothing, just couldn't sleep."

Darkness slipped back out under the tent flaps and into the gray grasses.

Matt sighed and sat up, rubbing his eyes. "Scared to sleep out here buddy?"

Charlie took a deep breath. "A little bit. It's so different. The sounds and the smells. Strange kinds of things, swamps, oyster shells."

"Not like Kansas, huh Charlie? When I first came to live with Grannie a couple of years ago, after Ma died, I couldn't sleep alone for weeks."

"Your mom is dead?"

"Yep."

"I'm sorry. I don't know anyone who's mom isn't around. Do you miss her?"

"All the time. But in different ways now. She was gone so suddenly. I had to move here with Pa. Because he didn't take good care of me, I moved in with Grannie."

"Will I meet your dad?"

"Maybe. He comes and goes. Does some shrimping, but

does a lot of gambling over Biloxi way too. He's always looking for easy money is what Grannie says."

"So you missed your mom when you moved here?"

"Still do. I had lots of trouble sleeping. Figured it might have been that I was always with Ma. Always just me and her before...well...before she died. She would kiss me goodnight, shut the light out and close the door. But I could still hear her fussing out in the kitchen, cleaning up. Or turning on the television and putting the volume lower. The squeak of the old chair as she sat down and put up the footrest. Familiar sounds."

Sounds like Mom makes at home too Charlie thought. When she isn't mad about something. "But didn't your grandmother kiss you good night and make night sounds?"

"Oh sure, she'd kiss me good night. But then she'd go right to bed too. Just silence. So I'd lay there and try to imagine Ma was there...right there in the other room watching TV. That's mostly when I'd cry. It was a hurt in the gut kind of missing. Knowing I'd never get her good night kiss again or hear her night sounds again. Never ever see her shut the door or turn out the light again. Never...ah you know what I mean."

Charlie felt his sad face coming. Don't cry Charlie. You can feel bad for Matt, but don't cry. Pinching his nose to stop the burning made his eyes water. He shook his head to clear away the feelings, but that only made the first tear spill out. Dang. Glad Matt can't see me in the dark.

Matt said," So I started getting afraid of the dark. The

dark blackness before you fall asleep. But I got over it, grew out of it. I wanted to let you know, you aren't alone. Maybe when you are older like me, you won't be afraid either. Sure stinks until then."

"Yeah, sure does."

Matt lay back down, folding his arms behind his head. "Good night, Charlie. If you want to know any tricks to help you fall asleep just ask me. Okay?"

"Thanks, Matt."

"No problem buddy. See you in the morning."

"See ya'."

With those few words said, Charlie felt better. So Matt used to be afraid of the dark? Mom always tells me to get to bed and turn on a night light if I need it. And Dad is gone to meetings and conventions and stuff. He doesn't even know I lie awake late at night. Used to be able to sneak in and sleep on the floor in their room. But they don't let me anymore, especially now when Mom's so strange with the morphemes or homrones or whatever Dad says come along with having a baby.

I'll get over this...yes I will. And when I do I'll sleep anytime and anywhere I please.

So Charlie laid back down. His mind drifted to the treasure map.

The breathing wind stilled and dark stayed out of the tent.

21

LILLIA

I listened for the twelfth chime to ring before I left the apartment. With Charlie camping out I don't have to worry about him sneaking up on me again. I wanted to ask the girls about the note I found in the antique room, and about old barn and the man.

Entering the back hallway, I paused to let my eyes adjust to the darkness. Moonlight brightened the scene outside the window.

I could see the barn, now back to a vine covered, falling apart building. I'd spent the last hours trying to figure out what the imagining might mean. I couldn't help but think I was supposed to see the package being hidden in the barn. If a clue is in the wooden box, I might have to try to find it. Or maybe it was a random imagining? Not connected with what the watching Pirate Queen needs to hear?

As I turned the corner I heard," Lillia! We are so glad to see you again. Where were you last night?"

Now I loved this kind of imagining! Miriam was braiding Emily's hair. Nell and Eleanor were playing checkers.

"I came too soon and you weren't here. So tonight I waited until the twelfth chime," I told the sisters. "Do any of you ever see other people who used to live here?"

The girls all started giggling and looking at each other. "Oh sweet Lillia, all the time!" Eleanor said. "Right now there are the four of us. But we have brothers and sisters you have not met."

"Have you seen the man who lived in the old house before your father bought it?"

"Oh yes," Nell said. "He has such a cute doggie."

"Do you know Mairead?" I asked.

Emily looked puzzled. "I am not sure. Who is she?"

Miriam said, "Be still sister, I am almost done. We have had others come through once in a great while. Others like you who can see us like you do, but I don't recognize that name."

Nell was hopping up and down in her seat. "Oh! Oh! Eleanor, who was that man? The one that mama was reading to us? The man who said things about imagination?"

Eleanor bit her lip, and narrowed her eyes. "Hmm, I know what you are talking about. That quote about real things and imaginary things. Who was he?"

Miriam said, "It was the French philosopher Jean-Jacques Rousseau. He said that the world of reality has limits but the world of imagination is boundless. Is that the one you mean? There, all done Emily."

Nell grinned. "That was it! Mama wants us to have a good education so she teaches us things like that."

Boundless! I liked that. No limits. Sometimes limits can feel safe, though. The big world can be scary. Like when I imagined my sister Chloe as a baby doll inside Mom. I stopped and scolded myself. Don't go down that path now Lillia.

I asked, "Miriam, are you going to do the Ouija Board again tonight?"

"We cannot. Mama took it away. She said it is the devil's tool. Papa told her it is just a game. However, she still saw fit to remove it. We know she hid it in the study. We hope Mama settles down and Papa will get it out again."

Eleanor said, "Was there something you wanted to ask the Ouija Board?"

"I guess I would ask Laurens about how to help the Pirate Queen Anne. I'm supposed to be using my abilities. But I don't know where she is. I'm not very good at this imagining power of mine."

"Our brothers are good at imagining," Nell said. "Especially Ira, he is always playing cowboys and Indians, or soldier. He loves to go to the mystery fort to pretend."

"What's the mystery fort?" I asked.

"An old foundation in the woods," Emily answered.

"When teachers talk about the history of this area, like how French explorers came here and how the Indians lived here but were moved out, they sometimes walk their classes over to the lost fort and teach the history lesson right there."

"No one is sure how old it is or who built it, thus it is a mystery," Miriam said. "I know children have been playing around it forever."

Maybe I'd check that mystery fort out. Sounded interesting.

I asked the girls if they ever pretended, maybe imagining they were princess's in a castle? They all started talking at once about how much fun they have pretending they live in a castle. How the horse hitching posts pull their carriages. How the grounds beneath the big trees become ballrooms with roofs made of Spanish moss.

"The statues are guardians of the kingdom. Except for the beautiful statue holding the bowl. She is our fairy godmother. We find notes in her bowl, from another kingdom, or a prince," Nell said. "It's magical."

"Mama puts them in her bowl," Miriam said, dismissively shaking her head at her sister.

"She does not."

"Does too."

The girls started quite a go-round about the fairy godmother statue. I could still hear their voices even as their figures faded away.

I glanced out the window toward the statue they had

argued about. In the moonlight, it appeared like something was lying in the bowl she held.

I raced down the unlit stairs, out the back door and around the side of house. I slid to halt as I neared her.

Catch your breath. Calm down. I took the last few steps toward her.

The small bowl did hold something! I took a deep breath and reached over the bowl as if I was playing the game Operation. Careful not to touch anything else, I pinched the edge of the paper and pulled it out...

My place has been marked
On maps by many dreamers.
Hoping to find pirate treasure,
Poor stupid schemers.

I will never leave the lonely ground,
Ever guarding what lies buried there.
For those who dare disturb the mound,
You have been warned...beware!

22

MYSTERY FORT

Early the next morning three adventurers set out on the Bon Secour River. Charlie on a mission to add clues to Captain Jack's pirate treasure map. Matt just glad to get Grannie's boat out on the river. Lillia there because Matt knew how to find the mystery fort.

The brackish water of the side channel moved silently, slipping away from the boat's prow as it pushed through. Trees, both alive and dead, hung out across the channel, secreting the passage of the small craft. Wet and tangled foliage hid the shoreline as the boat slipped past.

It had been a few minutes since they left the broad river to enter this narrower channel when Lillia asked, "Are you sure this is the right way?"

Matt said, "Yep I am. The mystery fort even shows up on the Captain Jack's map, right after the Snake Back curve."

Charlie, holding the map open on his lap, glanced up the river ahead and excitedly proclaimed, "That's it, the channel curves up ahead, just like Snake Back on the map. You were right Matt!" He stood, causing the boat to start rocking. Lillia yanked him back down.

"Watch out, you'll tip us over," she said sharply. "You can't bounce around in here like you do everywhere else."

"Sorry!"

"Are we close to the mystery fort Matt?" Lillia asked.

"Yep, we need to go through these curves and then around a big boulder sticking out. It's up ahead not too far. Charlie, is the big boulder on the map?"

Charlie glanced back down. "Might it be this mark called Skull Head?"

"That sounds about right. It's a bleached whitish gray color and looks like a big round bone."

Charlie felt the river banks were closing in on them, impeding their movement. The stream narrowed to flow through the sharp bends.

The Skull Head rock fit its name, except for the green goopy slime that clung to the edge near the water. Charlie shivered as they crept past.

Matt maneuvered along the left shore, his eyes scanning the bank. "This looks like a good place to pull off."

Lillia grabbed a tree that hung out over the bank. She tried to steady the tippy little boat as Charlie and Matt got out.

Charlie pointed. "Look back downriver. It twists right out of sight and the entrance disappears."

"Ah guys, how's about a hand here?" Lillia said, as the boat threatened to float away. She had one leg on the shore and one in the boat. "I'm on my way to doing a split if you don't help me. And I don't do splits!"

"Ooops sorry." Matt squatted on the bank and reached for the edge of the boat to steady it. "Here ya go. I got her. Boat's not going anywhere."

Lillia struggled, almost sliding back into the green murky water, before steadying herself and getting both feet on the bank. "There's no way I want to slip into that water. Can't even see a few inches in. Little fishies to bite my toes and big old gators right behind them."

Matt said, "The fort's foundation is just in the woods a little way, right by a grove of live oaks."

"I'm going to head up there and check it out. You two stay nearby, okay?" Lillia said.

"Don't be gone too long, we want to go further up this channel," Charlie said to Lillia as she started pushing through the brush growing at the river's edge.

"Don't worry Charlie. You'll get there," Lillia called back over her shoulder, as she pushed branches aside.

A little way in she lost sight of the boys, but could still hear them talking. Ahead the live oaks rose above the lower shore trees.

A clearing opened up for her. In it was a low wall, only a foot or so high, forming a large rectangle. She saw the irregular edges, worn oddly, unevenly. Small pieces of oyster shells could be seen poking out here and there.

The quiet was broken by the loud screech of a black bird. It flew up and off overhead. She instinctively ducked her head and shielded it with her arm. When she looked back up, walls were rising from the crumbling foundation.

23

LILLIA

I was rooted to the spot. The sky darkened. My feet, solidly anchored to the ground, held me captive to the scene of the building forming in front of me...right on top of the old tabby foundation that had been sitting there all along.

Through the thick wavy window glass, I saw light flickering. Smoke rising from the chimney brought the smell of burning wood.

A group of three figures approached from my right. They moved silently through the trees. Tall, dark skinned, with sleek black hair. Indians! They wore beaded buckskin vests. Soft leather leggings hugged their legs and moccasins covered their feet.

They kept walking toward the house, stopping just outside the door to the building.

I saw a boy clinging to the neck of the tallest Indian.

Mewling like a frightened, hurting kitten. His blond curly haired head tucked up under the Indian's brown skinned, square jaw. The dirt streaked shirt of the boy was torn and his short pants were caked with mud. He curled himself up in a fetal position, tight against the Indian's chest.

One of the men tapped lightly on the door of the building and stepped back.

It opened and a man appeared in the doorway. A little girl hid behind him, peering at the strange group who stood outside her door.

"Who is it Henri?" a female voice called from inside.

The man in the door pushed against the child clinging to his leg, moving her back into the house, as he said, "Stay inside. I'll take care of this." Without taking his eyes off the group, he grabbed a long shotgun from inside the cabin. He took a step out and closed the door, putting it between his family and the threat before him.

One of the Indians raised his hand, open palm out, trying to show he was coming in peace

I watched as Henri slowly raised the shotgun to his shoulder and leveled it at the strangers who'd arrived on his doorsteps.

My heart raced as I saw him cock the gun and get ready to shoot. "What do you want?" he said.

The Indian patted the boy's back before gently unwrapping one of the tiny arms from around his neck.

"Stop. Don't move," Henri commanded.

The boy jerked at the harsh words, grasped at the Indian and burrowed back deeper under his chin.

Henri motioned with his gun for the side two Indians to step back. They did.

He said, "Boy, look at me."

The boy raised his head, his blonde curls ghostly pale against the Indian's black hair. His muddy face streaked with tear tracks.

He opened his eyes wide when he saw the gun pointed at him. He whispered, "Please don't hurt us."

"Put the boy down," Henri said.

The Indian again gently pulled the boy's arm from around his neck. The boy peeked up at him with questioning eyes. He pulled the child's other arm off. The boy turned to look directly at the man with the gun and said, "Don't shoot. They are my friends. They saved me."

"Saved you from what boy?"

The young boy said, "From being buried alive by pirates." He sniffed and blinked his eyes. "I think my friend is dead. He tried to save me."

Henri gasped. He lowered his shot gun and motioned for the boy to come to him.

I let my breath out...feeling such relief. I watched the Indian set the boy down on the ground. He seemed about Charlie's age.

The Indian softly prodded the boy to go to the man. He took tentative steps toward Henri, before turning to glance back. The tall Indian shook his head side to side and motioned the child to keep going. He ran back to give the kind-faced, brown man a hug around his legs, then faced Henri and walked toward his new home.

I heard Charlie calling my name. The sunshine had returned, throwing dappled light to the grasses around me.

"I'll be right there."

Had I just seen Anne's son? He didn't die. He lived! After the imagining in the antique room, I thought the whole family was killed. I bet Anne doesn't know that. She still stands guard over the site where she thinks her son was buried alive. She warned me to leave her alone. I need to let her know her son lived! But how can I prove it to her?

24

LEAVING HANK

Back at the Tin Roof, Cecelia was finishing up with the lunch crowd. Her back had been aching again and she figured it won't be many more years she could keep this up. Lordy, but she missed her daughter Stella, gone almost three years. Cecelia had pictured being retired up in Mobile by now. Had to keep going a few more years. Needed to keep the boy in school and in clothes until he got a job and helped out some.

Matt seemed to be adjusting okay. No help from that no good father of his. Where in tarnation had Hank gone to yesterday? Promised he'd go along with the youngin's out on the tour, then never showed up.

Hank let the door slam behind him when he came in the Tin Roof.

"Well lookie who shows up? Was just thinking about you. Where'd you disappear to yesterday you no good weasel? And on top of it, some old bum is yelling about you right in front of Matt. How many people you owe money to now?"

"Ah stop your yapping. I told you I might have to help unload some extra boats for Tommy. Never promised I would make it for sure Miss Cecelia. I was tired after working and went and took a nap under a big old tree on that back road."

"He's your son. Good thing I didn't tell him you was coming along on cruise. Would have been a big disappointment again. Just like all the other times."

"You and Stella made sure I didn't see him for years. Why's it so important now all a sudden?" Hank grumbled.

"He's been asking after you is why. He wants to know where you were off to when he was little. I try to tell him don't pay you no never mind but he needs a father. Lord knows you ain't much of one, but you're the only one he's got. You could sober up and get a decent job if you wanted to. Be a good example for him. Not the bum you've been all of his life so far. You need to value the only treasure you got." Cecelia felt her blood pressure rising. No good came of letting that happen.

"Being called a bum don't make a man feel good Miss Cecelia. Why you known I've tried over the years. Like yesterday. I wanted to go, but I owed some money and I had a chance to do some work. Isn't that what you want? Me working?"

Why did she even put out the energy arguing with him?

He was a small, selfish, lazy man. It was a wasted effort. She turned her back and walked into the kitchen leaving Hank standing and staring after her.

Hank called out, "Just so you know, I got some bait and was gonna take Matt and his new friend fishing."

Coming back through the swinging door carrying a stack of clean napkins, Cecelia said, "That would have been a swell idea, but the boys are off exploring upriver. Wish you'd give a call, and plan ahead once in a while. Always switching, changing plans."

"What's upriver?"

"They are playing with a buried treasure map they got somewhere. Kid stuff. Keeping 'em busy, though."

"A map? Where'd they get it?"

"I don't know. Maybe on the cruise? Or from Pete? They were talking about visiting with him yesterday."

"Don't the new boy stay in the big house?"

"Thank you and come again," Cecelia called out to the last customers as they left, before answering Hank. "Yes he does and I don't want to hear any more from you about old papers, secret journals, and hidden drawers at the big house. You leave that boy Charlie alone. And you leave them nice house ladies there alone. Don't go asking him and his sister to sneak you in the house or some such nonsense. You hear me, Hank? I get wind of you bugging them to get in the house and I'll kick you right across Mobile Bay and on into Mississippi."

Hank sulked out of the restaurant. He started down the

road toward his trailer home back in the forest. That's what the boys must have been up to last night when I saw them walking back from the river. They musta been talking with Pete, that nosey old coot. Would have sneaked up and listened by their tent, but that gal would have seen me.

Need to find Matt and see what he's up to.

25

LILLIA

I started worrying about how much longer we were going to be out here. "Charlie, if you don't see what you are looking for soon we'll have to give up for today."

"A little further, please Lillia?"

Matt was shaking his head. "I don't know about this. It was a dream wasn't it? What's that dream got to do with us finding buried treasure that probably doesn't exist anyway? I think she's right, we should turn around."

"Promise we'll try another day?"

Matt turned the rudder and the boat spun quickly pointing back toward the main river.

"Hey! Warn us," Charlie said, grabbing the side of the boat.

"Oops, sorry buddy."

Charlie looked bummed. Too bad I thought. Him and his dreams. He'd told me about this one. I try to get interested but he just goes on and on so I tune him out sometimes.

I had to think and think hard. What could I possibly say to a mother ghost to convince her that her son wasn't buried where she thought he was? And with what Mairead told me about the danger, I had to be smart about how I did this. Not just rush in like I did at Land Between the Lakes.

Oh, why can't I just enjoy the sisters and meet their dressmaker? See them in their beautiful new clothes? Sit on the yard and sip tea with them? Play castles and kingdoms?

"I think I see some light ahead," Matt said. But before we could get out of the channel we had to push through drippy wet stuff hanging over the entrance. It did everything it could to hamper our efforts.

Once out on the river, Matt pointed us toward home and revved up the engine.

It stalled, sputtered a few times, and died.

Matt stood and reached for the cord to pull and start it again.

Nothing.

Again he tried.

Nothing.

I felt an icy chill wind. Small waves seemed to pick up, swirling, starting to turn our boat sideways. I looked for a larger boat that might have caused the river to twist like this. No one else was around us.

On the river bank, a section of trees started swaying and churning.

The current turned us completely around twice and then we stopped, pointing toward the channel…the one we had just clawed our way out of. From it came a strange greenish fog. Low lying. Crawling from the opening.

We were speechless. Our shallow breaths the only sound.

The fog crept further out. It grew.

"Let's get out of here! I've never ever seen anything like that!" Matt reached to pull the motor again and it started with a roar. He opened the throttle and pointed us downriver.

I caught sight of the fog being suddenly sucked back into the channel. The trees stopped swaying. The entrance was again hidden.

26

BURIED ALIVE

*T*hree hundred years earlier...

The Indians hiding in the forest watched as the greenish, low-lying fog crept across the dull leather boots of the bearded man, the peg leg of the bent old man, and the delicate cloth slippers of the young boy. It slithered over the freshly dug hole and across the shoulders of the two men inside the earthen tomb. Then it wrapped itself around a large leather chest sitting at the furthest edge of the pit.

Grunts of exertion came with each spade full of wet dirt tossed out of the hole.

"Ain't this deep enough Bones?"

"Shut up. I'll tell ye when it's done," Bones said.

Trembling and shivering, the young boy cried and clung to the old man.

"Quit your blathering you little girlie boy. Your daddy gave you that blonde sissy hair and your mama dressed you up all fancy like."

"Leave the boy alone. Do what you want to me but take him back to the ship. Return him to his mother and father. He's an innocent," the peg-legged man said. "Take me, I'm an old crippled man."

"Innocent? No blood of that wretch is innocent so shut your mouth. Neither of you is worth any trouble. You heard what the captain said."

"Now Bones? Is it deep enough now? We're getting tired in here."

Bones lifted his lantern out over the pit. The fog glowed and throbbed in the light. He nodded.

The two diggers emerged and grabbed hold of the side handles on the chest. With loud grunts and much cursing, they managed to lower it down the freshly dug hole.

"Come here little laddie," Bones said. The evil grin on his face was lit by the lantern now sitting on the ground.

"Leave the lad go back to the ship. He doesn't know where he is. He'll not tell anyone what's here," pleaded the bent old man.

Bones spoke to the boy again, more forcefully. "Come here I said."

"Run! Run as fast as you can," shouted the old man,

pushing the boy away toward the dark forest. "Don't look back!"

Without hesitation, the boy was grabbed by Bones and tossed into the hole, on top of the chest.

"No," the old man screamed before he was smacked across the back of the head with one of the spades and tumbled in on top of the boy.

Bones said," Hargh. The Captain was right. Dead men tell no tales."

Back to now...

Charlie asked, "What happened out there? Did you all see the creepy, crawly, green fog-like stuff?"

"I did," Matt answered. He shut off the motor and started tying Cecelia's little boat to the dock. "Weird looking, but probably just some swamp gas reflecting the sun."

"Swamp gas? Listen to you. You don't even know what you're talking about. There's no such thing," a short, skinny, dirty looking man said as he took a drag of his cigarette.

With a nod toward the small man, Matt said, "My pa, Hank."

"Been out fishing?" Hank asked.

Matt finished securing the boat. "No, just cruising around."

"I'm Charlie. Nice to meet you, Hank," Charlie said, extending his hand.

Surprised and caught off guard, Hank tossed his

cigarette stub into the river and reached to shake Charlie's hand.

"Lillia visited the mystery fort and Matt and I were going to explore with our pirate map from Captain Jack," Charlie explained.

"That stupid goof? You shoulda come to me. I could have told you a thing or two."

Matt rolled his eyes and helped Lillia up out of the boat. "Pa, leave us alone. We don't need help. We're just pretending. Playing around."

Charlie was hurt. He wasn't playing around. What if they did find a treasure? Dad had shown him a newspaper article that about a guy in California who found a can full of old gold coins on his property. You never know.

"Never mind him, boy, he's always so serious. So you saw the green fog, heh?"

"We did," Charlie piped up. "What is it? I thought it might mean something. It came to me in a dream too."

"It means you're on to something. Best I remember ever hearing about it was from an old shrimper. He bragged about seeing the green fog and finding gold coins washed up among the swamp grass. Never found a treasure site."

Matt shook his head. "Pa, stop telling your tall tales."

Hank took note of Charlie's interest. This was the boy living in the big house. Stories of pirate maps kept in journals there might or might not be true. Couldn't hurt to get on the kid's good side. Might get me in the house to snoop around.

"What you boys say I take you out tomorrow and we do some real buried treasure hunting? Not waste any more time playing around? Don't even need that pretend map. I know this area like the back of my hand. I can show you river channels you ain't never finding on your own."

"Leave him alone Pa," Matt said.

With a threatening glare, Hank said, "I told you I'll take you out tomorrow boy." He relaxed his face, turned his lips up in the corners and faced Charlie. "How about that kid? Let me show you the hidden places."

Charlie looked over at Matt. "Would that be alright? Couldn't hurt."

Matt clenched his fists and watched as his father sent a big sneering grin in his direction. The ugly gaps where teeth were missing in full view now.

Lillia said, "Right now we have to get home. Grauntie will be waiting for us." And with that, she gave Charlie a little push and all three walked away.

Hank watched them leave. Snotty little girl. Not even saying goodbye.

27

LILLIA

I followed the road back up to the big house. Matt and Charlie tagged along behind me. What a piece of work that Hank was. A grown man making like he can find buried treasure. I mean really! The boys pretending was one thing, but Hank leading Charlie on like that was wrong. The whole pirate thing was getting a little over done.

Grauntie and the boys left to meet Myra at the Tin Roof for dinner. I needed some quiet time, to try and make sense of the imagining at the mystery fort today, which of course I didn't mention to anyone. My imaginings seem to confuse and concern people. They sure confuse me. And I know how much they concern Mom. She never got over me, a little four-year-old, telling her there was both a dolly and a baby in her tummy. Soon after Mom and Dad discovered Chloe hadn't lived long enough to be born. It was a sad time in our family.

I walked through the house. Trying to open my senses...to let the past form...to get a clue. Anything to help solve the mystery of Anne...where she was...what she needed to hear.

I sat on the sofa in the front parlor, running my hands over the brass tacks on the edges of the arms, fingers feeling the weave pattern of the beautiful rose and gold colored fabric. I closed my eyes. Open to anything coming to me. Minutes went by. Nothing came.

I peeked in the antique room, but all was quiet there too.

This was getting frustrating. I'm supposed to be this imagineer and I don't know how to control it...how to make an imagining happen.

I walked outside. I know! I'll go to the barn and see if I can find what the Creole man hid in there. I smiled as I remembered getting sniffed out by a dog from a different time. Dogs have a strong sense of smell, but across decades of time?

I grabbed a branch and swatted at the tall grasses I had to walk through. I hate you snakes, so I'm warning you to get out of my way. I felt like a pioneer breaking a trail.

Lucky me, the barn door hung lopsided, leaving a gap just big enough for me to slide through.

Shafts of dusty light angling down to the earthen floor came through the open spaces between the wall boards. Dry heavy air, choking, suffocating. I don't want to stay in here too long.

Darn, times I wish I wasn't quite so short. I'll need something to stand on to reach the area between the beam and the roof slope. Nothing looked promising until I spied two sturdy wooden crates behind some old rakes. If I was careful I should be able to stack them and stand on them.

The crates wobbled as I climbed on them. I couldn't see, but now I could reach high enough to feel along the ledge. Grainy, rough, brittle surface. My groping kicked up more ancient dust. I started sneezing and had to lean fully against the boards to steady myself. There didn't seem to be anything on the shelf.

I decided to feel along just a little further. My fingers ran up and over a cool, smooth, metal surfaced object. I couldn't figure out what the shape was. Pushing it closer to the edge, I tried to see it.

It teetered on the edge then crashed to floor with a thud. An ax head had almost hit me! I'd better give up before I got hurt out here.

You are the imagineer for sure Lillia. Just not good at imagining what you need to. So much for this barn producing any clues.

I walked back toward the house. Across the yard stood three statues and one empty pedestal. What happened to that other little guy? Kind of like my family...me, Charlie, our new little sister or brother coming soon, and the missing Chloe.

Homesickness hit...missing Mom and Dad. Missing the sister I never got to meet. Missing the family life, we could have had…with Chloe alive and Mom and Dad happy together.

28

DREAMING

The morning came in lazy and slow. The air heavy and oppressive with warm moisture. There was a dullness to it. People slowed down as they moved through the mugginess. They spent the day hoping a cool lifting breeze would come with the evening.

Charlie woke up. He could hear the tour guides coming in for the start of their day. He had dreamt a lot last night. Grandpa once told him to stay still a minute when you wake up and try to remember your dreams.

He had said, "Charlie, your dreams open passageways between the conscious and unconscious minds."

"I have more than one mind, Grandpa?"

"Sort of. Do you know what conscious means?"

"Alive?"

"Sort of. It's the part of your brain that you use when you're awake," he said.

"So when do I use the other one?"

"The unconscious or subconscious mind is the oldest, deepest part of your brain. Most people only use it when they are asleep."

"Why should I remember my dreams? What does it matter?"

"The Native American Indians place a high value on dreams. They allow the old inner part of your brain to speak. So if you are trying to figure something out, an answer might appear in a dream. Be still, pieces of your dream linger for a bit. If you can hold those pieces, even the tiniest thread of them, relax and follow that as far back as you can."

When Charlie went to sleep last night, he kept the pirate map in his head, hoping that his old inside brain would come up with some ideas where to find the treasure.

He dreamt he was floating on his back in a river. Above him in the sky, Chloe was flying, twirling and flipping around, while she tossed gold stars out of her hands. He felt himself sinking. The view of her above was fading away. Tiny, delicate air bubbles rose around him. He saw Matt float by underwater. In his dream, Charlie called out to Matt, but he just kept drifting down. Then Hank floated down past him. Then more bodies came, sinking faster… the last he remembered he was struggling to breathe, choking. He woke up to see that morning was lighting the sky.

Matt had decided yesterday that they should sneak out and leave before Hank found them. The two of them would head upriver to explore on their own. Better get going. Be positive. Today will be the day we find treasure.

Matt had been up for hours. He did not want to run into Pa. He would be sure to spoil a fun day. I don't care if the map or the treasure are real...what matters is my friend Charlie thinks they are.

Lillia had set up the guest register for tourists to sign.

"Glad they have the air-conditioning on today," Nora said, walking by fanning herself with one of the information pamphlets. "Imagine it'll be a slow day with this heat. Feels like not much will be going on today."

29

LILLIA

I wanted to get done early because last night I realized that if I saw the Indians bring the boy to someone living in the old fort, he probably had been rescued nearby. Maybe the site the Pirate Queen guarded was near where we'd been yesterday. I decided I'd find the boys and see if they'd take me back there.

And I sure hoped Charlie and Matt didn't try to go back on their own. From what Mairead said about Anne, exploring in those waters sounded dangerous.

I saw Hank lurking around the big house at lunch time. What a creepy feeling that guy gave me. Myra talked to him. He left right after that, heading down the old road to the pier. I figured Matt and Charlie must have ditched him today.

Just like Grauntie said, the tourists were few. The last one had come through over two hours ago. Some university students, who were involved with fixing the gardens, had worked in the morning, but were gone by noon.

The afternoon dragged by slowly. Tod from the pirate cruise didn't show up. Oh well…at least we had fun that one afternoon.

"Grauntie, do you know where Charlie is?"

"I'm not sure. He said he was going to be with Matt. Maybe they are up at the Tin Roof having ice cream?"

"I'm going to walk over and see if they're there. Okay with you?" I asked.

"Sure you go on. I don't think any more tours will be coming today. I'm going stay inside this cool house and start putting things away."

The heat hit me when I walked out. It took my breath away. No breeze at all.

Cecelia said she hadn't seen the boys, but she told me Hank had been in earlier looking for them too. He said they had made plans to go fishing or something on the river and the boys hadn't shown up. But that was over two hours ago.

"Do you have any idea where they would go fishing?"

"Well, it's always been pretty good down by the old pier," Cecelia said. "You take the old road from the big house and head out to the river. Right near the seafood processing plant."

"Charlie and I went down there one night. We met Pete the night watchman."

"Pete's one of the good guys. His family goes way back around these parts. He's what is called a Creole."

"What's that mean, Creole?"

"In these southern states, it usually means descended from original French settlers. Some people, especially in the Caribbean, consider you Creole if you have mixed European and black ancestors. All I know is, I love Creole food and music!"

"Do you cook that way here?"

"For sure. The Tin Roof serves some great Creole style dishes. And I remember Amelia, one of the Swift girls. Lordy but that Meme could make a mean seafood gumbo. She had a restaurant right here in Bon Secour named after her, Meme's. Her recipes are in a book they sell up at the big house."

So Amelia, called Meme, was a sister I hadn't met. "Thanks, Cecelia. If you see the boys tell them we're having a farewell party tonight. Though, secretly, with this heat, I hope it's an indoor one!"

Starting back toward the house I felt like someone was following me. I turned to glance over my shoulder. No one.

Hmm, oh well. I turned and jumped. There stood Hank right in front of me, cigarette hanging out of his mouth.

"Hey there miss. How's your day going?"

I shuttered. "Fine, excuse me. Grauntie's expecting me back soon."

He started to move aside to let me pass, but then I felt the touch of his hand on my arm. "Have you seen my son and your brother? We was going to go do some exploring. Must have got our wires crossed. Can't seem to find them."

I moved away from him as I said, "Nope. Haven't seen them."

"You looking for them too ain't ya?"

I tried to ignore him.

"We'll see who finds them first. Sort of like a game. You like to play games don't ya?" He dropped his cigarette on the road and ground it out with the toe of his old boots. His eyes caught mine, and he gave me an odd smile before turning to walk away.

30

GOING ALL IN

The late afternoon brought no relief from the humidity and heat.

Hank hated days like this, especially when he was stuck. And he was stuck for sure. He had people looking for him, people he owed money to. Where in damnation was that son of his? Supposed to meet the kids at the dock this morning.

He had walked around the big house trying to find the kid until the nosy old bitty asked him if she could help him. Like he was scaring off tourists or something. They thought they were such a big deal. Spending all that money on saving some old house.

Hank walked over to Tin Roof to find them and then had to face Cecelia and all her chatter.

He wasn't no fool. He had his doubts about buried treasure. But hey he had doubts but a whole bunch of stuff.

Like winning big at the casino. But you can't win if you don't gamble. Same with the treasure. You ain't gonna find if you don't seek.

Getting on the right side of Charlie would help. He could play with the boy's mind. Hank could tell he was an easy mark. The girl not so much. He got strange feelings from her. Too uppity. Bet she wouldn't even tell them he was looking for 'em.

And now darn that brat, Matt. He and the kid ditched me. So I ain't the perfect pa. He ain't the perfect kid. Bet they went up the river without me. They can't hide from me all day.

* * *

Matt and Charlie had been exploring for hours now. Matt was confused as to why he couldn't find the opening again.

"It's a sign of something that the green fog appeared," Charlie said.

"The fog probably looked green cause it was reflecting all the grasses and vines and stuff around it," Matt said.

"But your dad said a shrimper found gold coins in this area."

"Yeah well, Pa can say lots of things. He told Ma things that weren't true just to get her to stay with him and support him so he could lay around."

"But Matt, this might be something different."

"He just wants us to take him out to hunt for treasure.

And there isn't buried pirate treasure anywhere near here. Maybe not anywhere ever."

Charlie was crestfallen. "Captain Jack said there was a treasure. He would know."

Matt slowly shook his head side to side. "He runs a silly pirate cruise taking people on tours for money. The more he plays the pirate thing out, the more they love it. Good gig for him."

"That's a mean thing to say."

"Don't get me wrong. I like the guy. In fact, I might work for him on busy days. Help with the ship. But it's make believe."

"What about Pete? He said there was treasure too."

"And Pete says he sees ships come up to that old wharf. He says he can describe them in detail and make them come alive in his memory. He's probably imagining buried treasure too. Don't you get it, Charlie? They are all dreamers. Except for Pa only dreams. At least Jack works at playing pirate. And Pete has a job too. Pa doesn't care about you and me Charlie. He only cares about finding easy money."

"But Matt, aren't you my friend? Aren't we trying to find treasure?"

"Sure Charlie, I'm your friend and we're running around having fun together. But it's like playing Star Wars or Ninja Turtles. Only a game."

Charlie couldn't believe what he was hearing. He knew

the difference between pretend and real. He believed there was treasure here.

Matt started backpedaling when he saw Charlie's face fall.

"You didn't let me finish. At first, I thought it was pretend...a game. But yesterday, with the fog and the swirling water and all I started changing my mind. You got me believing too."

Charlie took a long look at Matt and said, "Really? You're not just saying that now?" He sat up taller and cleared his throat. "Cause you don't have to help me."

"No, I like you. I like your spirit. You go all in. Let's go check again and see if we can find that entry to the mystery fort channel. I mean we just took it yesterday. Those things don't just disappear."

So one more time, the little fishing boat motored along the edges of the Bon Secour, with two young treasure hunters searching for the disguised opening to the hidden channel. On this try they found it.

Pushing aside tall swamp grasses and low hanging branches, they struggled to get inside where the river branch would open up more. They ducked their heads but the wet vegetation reached out, slapping against them.

And then they were gone from the river, swallowed up. The grasses and overhanging branches filled back the opening once again, hiding the passageway.

31

LILLIA

I saw traces of the old original wharf, pilings sticking proudly out of the water.

I could imagine the double-decker steamer, Bella, docking here. Gangplank coming down, ladies in long dresses and bonnets being helped off by courteous men in straw hats. The seamstress walking off, her bolts of the latest fabrics from some far away city being unloaded.

Workers were leaving the seafood plant a little way down the river.

Some clouds had moved in, but it didn't feel like rain. The wind seemed to be picking up, things might cool off in time for the farewell party planned for tonight.

Maybe the watchman had seen the boys. That old looking place with the front porch must be his.

I knocked and heard a call from inside. "Come on in." Hesitantly I opened the screen door and stepped in. It was like a museum in here. Not at all what I'd expected. Models of ships carefully displayed on simple plank shelves. Black and white photographs hung on all the walls.

"Hey there young lady, have you enjoyed your visit to our beautiful part of the world?"

"Yes, it's nice here. By the way, my name is Lillia. You've got some pretty cool things in here."

"Thank you. Local history is a real interest of mine. Your brother and Matt have been here a couple of times and seemed to enjoy it as well."

"They have? Wondering if you've seen them today."

"I did. I finished my shift and was sitting here on my porch enjoying a little toast and coffee. The boys stopped in to say hi. They said they were taking Cecelia's boat out again to check on something you all had seen yesterday. Something about a green fog near the mystery fort."

My face must have given away my concern because he asked me if anything was wrong. I explained how no one knew they had taken off or where they had gone.

"It does seem like a long time for them to be on the river. The boat isn't back so they must still be exploring. Tell you what, I don't start work for a while. What do you say to you and me take a little cruise up the river and see if we can find them?"

"That might be a good idea, Pete. I appreciate it. I'm worried about them."

"Just give me a couple of minutes. I'll be right back," Pete said.

I thought about letting Grauntie know I was heading out but decided not to. No need having her worry too.

The sun's beams bounced off the glass from a framed paper across the room. In a cheap, silver frame, hanging at a slight tilt, was a poem. The paper was yellowed, showing deep creases and a few small water spots. The glass covering it had a light film of dust.

Curious, I walked over to read the poem...

When you hear this mother,
I don't know where I'll be,
The words said by another,
But know they come from me.

A simple little rhyme,
You often said for fun.
You spoke this many a time,
Sweet whispers to your son,

I love you madly and forever,
You know this to be so,
So I will leave you never,
And you must never go.

I miss you Mother,
Love, Your son Laurent

Pete came back into the room. "Ready to go. Called and left a message with work that I'll be showing up a bit late."

I said," This poem is beautiful. Who is Laurent?"

"He's my ancestor. Someone in my family tree. I'm about the last branch now," Pete said with a chuckle. "Nik Coles found a box in the old barn. The poem was in it."

This was an interesting twist. I was reading a poem that might be from the packet I'd seen hidden in the barn decades ago. No wonder it wasn't there yesterday...it's here. I said, "So if this came from the old barn, why did he give it to you?"

"Well, a great great uncle of my used to live there. Thomas Gavin. He built the house that the Swift's bought in 1902."

"I heard about him. So you're related to the Gavin's?"

"Sure am. And I have descendants that lived in this area since the late 1600's."

"Pete, did any of your relative's live in a place called the mystery fort?" I asked.

He thought a moment before saying, "Could of I guess. Historians around here never could figure out just who built that foundation or when. I imagine any structure built in those days didn't sit empty long before someone new moved in. Why?"

I answered, "Just curious." But thoughts were flying around in my head. Like the floaters Grauntie talked about.

I couldn't stop them, couldn't consider what they meant...they moved away, out of reach.

But I needed them to focus soon. And I needed to find Charlie and Matt soon. Something was coming and it was coming fast.

32

ANGRY HUNT

Hank cursed under his breath as he watched Lillia and Pete push off and head upriver.

So he'd been right to follow her. Look at them take off. Little liar. She says I don't know where they are and the boys must be home. She knows right where they are and she's taking that old buzzard with her to help dig up the treasure.

The gold is mine. I deserve it. I've been scrapping along my whole life.

Darn them. He couldn't lose them now. Think you dummy. What had that boy said? Mystery fort?

Seeing the old man's bike leaning against a tree nearby, Hank decided to borrow it for a little ride. That old crumbling foundation was right off the Simmon house road. He'd get there first and show them all he's not gonna be fooled with. Anything that's Matt's, is mine. I'm his pa.

Hank didn't see Cecelia, Myra, and Nora chatting out in front of the big house as he sped by. He didn't hear Cecelia call out to him either.

"Who was that?" Nora asked.

Cecelia shook her fist at him. "Matt's father. Hell bent on getting somewhere."

"Maybe he knows where the kids are?" Myra asked.

"I don't think so. He came to the Tin Roof right before Lillia. He was trying to find Matt and Charlie."

"I'm getting worried. I'm surprised they aren't back for the party." Nora said. "Charlie hasn't touched base with me all day long. Matt's a good kid, and I'm sure they are fine. Just would like to lay my eyeballs on them soon."

Cecelia said, "Well since we're pretty much done setting things up for your farewell party, what do you say we walk on over to Pete's place and see if Lillia and the boys might be there. She mentioned checking out if the boys were fishing at the old dock."

"Sure I'll go with. Who's Pete?" Nora asked.

Cecelia explained who Pete was as they walked down the overgrown road to the river.

* * *

Hank pedaled hard, tipping his head down to push against the strengthening winds. He almost missed the turn to the road to take him near the old foundation.

He passed the Simmon house. A wire-haired mutt came

racing from behind the house, and with a yapping and growling chased after him, nipping at his heels.

"Get you mongrel," Hank said, kicking at him with one foot. The dog stopped and stood taunt, his high pitched barking following after Hank.

A small marker showed him the path to the mystery fort. Soon the narrow bike tires were bogging down in the sandy soil. Tipping over, the bike landed on top of him. Hank cursed and kicked it away as he got up. He hurried down the path on foot.

In the shadows of the big oaks, he saw the foundation but moved quickly past it, heading in the direction he figured the branch of the river might be. He had to duck and push his way through the dense underbrush, thinking this wasn't at all like he'd remembered seeing it as a boy.

33

LILLIA

I hoped I could find the channel opening. The sun gave the entire water surface a blinding fiery glow. Trees were becoming black silhouettes on the shoreline.

I told Pete about the strange things that happened to the three of us on the river yesterday. "We explored a channel near here, came back out to the river, and that's when we saw the greenish creeping mist."

Pete was nodding. "You aren't alone in seeing a strange fog or mist. Not seen it myself, but I've heard tell of it."

"Really?"

"I always figured the fog was a fluke of nature, or lighting, or time of day."

"Hank told us someone found gold coins after the fog rolled out one time. Do you think that's really true?" I half wished it might be true. The thought of buried treasure nearby meant the Pirate Queen could have been in this area.

But then my little brother could be in danger trying to find it if that's where he and Matt went.

Pete said, "I don't like to bad mouth people, but that Hank is bad news in my opinion. To be honest, I've heard stories about coins being found, but don't know how true they are."

I decided to stick my neck out and ask Pete if he knew anything about a woman pirate.

"Strange you should ask. One of the stories about pirates and buried treasure, I've heard round these parts, did tell of a pirate lady. Heck, those fantasies keep Captain Jack in business!" Pete chuckled and slapped his knee. "Course anyone who ever gets caught on those narrow and confusing channels, and hears strange sounds can claim the Pirate Queen is chasing them away. Why are you asking?"

He just used the words Pirate Queen! That's what Laurens called Anne.

I felt like I couldn't do this alone anymore. It was getting too big for me. I needed help. So I told Pete everything I'd learned in the past few days.

I even told him about the verses I'd found. I had a feeling he wouldn't laugh at me and my imaginings. Or make me feel like I was just on the edge of crazy.

"These abilities you have sound pretty unique, but I know you're not alone in seeing ghosts. History has recorded many sightings. Hard to prove or disprove. You know I like to conjure up pictures of the past in my mind. I like to think I have a pretty strong imagination too."

I couldn't resist saying, "Isn't it fun sometimes?"

Pete said, "I love it Lillia! Just like you do. But right now, by the sounds of what you know, we need to find the boys. And the sooner the better."

I said, "You're right. I just want to get them out of harm's way. Thanks for listening Pete."

Pete gave me a thumbs up. "Right. Let's find those two boys and let them know they'll miss a fine party if they don't get back."

I felt the wind pick up again. Clouds moved in, their masses reflecting the glow from the sun as it settled nearer the horizon. The river no longer glistened and shimmered, instead, it took on a dull gold color. Small waves rocked us.

I searched the bank looking for the channel entrance.

I called out for Charlie. Pete shouted Matt's name. The thick air and the swirling wind sucked our calls away. Now the river's surface was bubbling.

"Pete, something doesn't feel right."

He shifted nervously, looking over one shoulder, then the other.

Suddenly we were tipping, being pushed to one side, our little boat listing precariously.

"What's going on?" Pete shouted. "I can't control the boat."

My mouth dropped open. I saw a ship rising out of the river.

Three tall masts, reaching out of the churning waters, held sails dripping with slimy, green weeds. With a shutter, the tattered, dirty cloths caught the wind and snapped open. The hull rose silently next to us. The prow extending out over our heads.

Atop the tallest mast flew a black and white flag...the skull and crossbones.

I saw Pete. His eyes were wide open and his mouth hung slightly open as he stared at the ship.

It passed through us. We were on the other side when I saw a small skiff being rowed toward shore.

A tall man stood in the small boat. In one hand he held up a lantern, while his other hand clasped the handle of a sword hanging at his side. His tangled and dirty hair hung out from under a greasy scarf wrapping his head. One foot, encased in a tall, leather boot, rested on the side of the vessel.

Through the thickening mist surrounding them, I made out four other figures. Two men were rowing and an old, hunched man sat in the skiff. Leaning against him, was a blonde curly haired boy.

I squinted trying to follow the strange vision but it disappeared in the thick fog.

34

BEWARE SHE SAID

Matt and Charlie pushed through the growth and were soon on their way through the Snake Back curves. Ahead Skull Head rock pushed out of the water.

Dead branches obstructed their travel. Putrid, rotting weeds floated past. Tangled, cold wetness enveloped them.

Matt turned off the motor, fearing the weeds would choke the propeller blades. The boat creaked. Somewhere overhead a gull called out, the sound echoing in the stillness. Then silence.

Charlie felt the coolness in the air. "I can't believe how dark it is in here," he said nervously.

"Clouds were coming out on our way here so the sun is probably just hidden." Matt didn't want Charlie getting too afraid, but he too wondered why everything seemed so dark suddenly.

"It's more than that. Look at the trees. They're making a roof over the river. They hide the sky."

Matt felt the same thing. Something was hiding us here today, but what?

"Which way is out Matt?"

Matt started to point behind him, the way they had come. It was different now. Like a pool, not a channel anymore.

"It's all so still," Charlie said. "How come? How come the water's not moving? No current?"

Matt realized that if you dropped him in here he couldn't tell you which way was back out. The water was covered in green slime that seemed like it hadn't moved in years.

"We're in backwater Charlie. No biggie. Bet this explains the green fog."

Charlie picked up on the nervousness in Matt's voice. "The wind might have stirred up the green gunk, mold or pollen or whatever to make that green fog, right Matt?"

The two boys realized they'd better pay attention to what was going on. Something was not right and they both felt it. Something strange was in the air.

Matt took one of the backup oars and poked it in the water. Shallow. He pushed off and the boat moved the green gunk aside.

Charlie watched the slime ooze back together behind the boat. He looked up and shouted, "Watch out."

A snake coiled around an overhanging branch, his head twisting and turning as it followed the boys progress.

Matt pointed, calling out, "Look Charlie! Behind Skull Head rock…it's starting to come over it."

The green fog slithered over the rock, smothering the stark grayness of the rock's surface. Speechless, they watched it approach them on the surface of the pool.

It stopped short of the boat, then started a slow retreat back over the rock and into the twisted grasses on the shore.

The boys followed with their eyes.

"Come on Matt. That is the spot," Charlie said in a low whisper.

Matt rowed them to the bank. They climbed out and Charlie reached back into the boat to get the shovels.

Now Hank heard voices. It was so thick here. He could barely push his way through. He swung himself up to the lower branches of a live oak, swatting at the Spanish moss threatening to tangle him up in its fibrous web.

He climbed higher, pulling himself awkwardly to the next branch. Gotta be easier here than in the darn underbrush he muttered. It'll be a long time before that kid of mine does anything like this again, making his old man sneak around looking for him.

No siree. Why should I have to do it all? Matt's too old

to run around pretend treasure hunting. Needs to start doing some work on the shrimp boats.

Hank finally stopped his climb. He hoped this was high enough to catch a glimpse of the boys before Pete and the girl found them. He lay across a limb, scooting out towards the end of it. Then, below him, he saw the boys.

They were trying to dig into the mucky ground. Hank leaned out further, to hear what they were saying. He heard Charlie say something about buried treasure. I knew it. They found it!

Hank almost lost his grip when something dark and moving fast, swooshed by him. His head swiveled. What kind of wind was that?

A high-pitched, keening wail tore through him.

Lordy, hang on old man. There's a hurricane a coming.

Hank saw Matt fall to the ground. What a ninny! Can't even stay on his feet in a little wind.

Then he watched the unbelievable scene of Charlie being lifted from the ground, shovel and all, and tossed into the slime at the edge of the water.

With that, Hank fell out of the tree.

35

LILLIA

I watched the strange group disappear into an opening on the river bank. Pete and I stared at each other.

Pete found his voice first and said, "What just happened? I sure hope the boys aren't out here now."

Without thinking, I called out, "Charlie?"

"Ahoy there, who goes below?" A voice boomed out from the pirate ship still looming over us.

Boom! A musket ball flew over our heads. Pete and I both dove for the deck. We stared wide-eyed, face to face.

As suddenly as it had appeared, the ship sank back under the water, leaving a completely flat, unmoving surface behind.

I peered over the side of our boat. It looked like we were once again alone on the Bon Secour River. But were we?

"Can you tell me what is going on Lillia? What do you know?"

I needed to find out how much Pete could see. I knew what I saw, but I'm getting used to seeing strange things that other people don't. "Ah, what did you see?" I asked him.

He hesitated before saying, "Pirates?"

I nodded. So we had a shared imagining! Like the one I'd had with Miss Margaret back in Kentucky. Only this was a lot scarier than bluegrass music!

"I believe you have some explaining to do young lady," he said. "You don't seem quite as shocked as me, by what we just saw."

"Remember my telling you I saw things, had imaginings? Well, that's what they look like. You were sharing my imagining. But right now we need to rescue the boys. I've got a feeling there's real trouble heading their way."

I was kicking myself for not taking Charlie's buried treasure talk more seriously. I just figured it was little kid stuff. I would have told him not to go looking without a grownup along. I hoped that this was all a big mix-up and Matt and Charlie were back at the Tin Roof having ice cream. But all my senses said they were down that channel and the Pirate Queen watched for their arrival.

We entered the channel the strange skiff had just gone into. The air thickened behind us, pushing further into the darkness. I need to focus...to find the spot we were at yesterday. This looked like it might be the Snake Back curve. It shouldn't be much further. This didn't feel good at all. Where are you Charlie? I don't want to go in here. I'm scared. I want to go back to the farewell party.

Then I saw them. Matt was lying on the ground. Charlie struggling in the muck and water. And was that Hank pushing himself up off the ground?

Screams filled the air around me...passing through me.

36

DROWNING

"Pa?"

"Just thought I'd drop in."

Matt said, "That's not funny! I'm scared Pa."

Hank pushed himself up to his hands and knees. "You think you're clever. Sneaking away to find the treasure. Well, lookie here, cause I'm…"

Something slammed Hank and pushed him up against a tree. He grunted. "What the heck is going on here?"

Matt crawled by, trying to reach Charlie struggling in the water. "I'm coming buddy."

"Boy, you come back here and help your Pa. I think I broke something." Hank watched Matt keep going. Suddenly Matt seemed to fling himself right in on top of Charlie. They both screamed, struggling to get free of the muck and weeds, but they were pushed under again.

Hank shook his head. This is crazy. What is going on?

Are they acting to get out of trouble? He shouted at them, "Okay boys, heads up out of the water. You've been under too long. Quit your horsing around." He wasn't going to be tricked by two conniving youngsters.

Even as the realization that they weren't fooling was coming to him, his body was flying through the air and he landed with a splash near the drowning boys. He felt a pressure pushing him down under the water. He fought against it. Flailing his arms, grasping for Matt. His boy was here too. He had to save him.

Underwater Charlie was losing consciousness. He was slipping into the dream. Chloe was above him, Matt slipping by…and there was Hank. The dream was coming true. Or was he asleep and dreaming it again?

"Charlie! Matt!" Lillia shouted. "We're almost to you. Hang on."

Pete ran their boat up on the shore and jumped out. He saw Hank struggling in the water, gasping for breath before going under again.

Pete grabbed for a hand that reached out. It slipped away from his grasp.

The top of a head rose part way out of the water. It was Matt. He tried gulping for air.

"We're here Matt," Pete pleaded, "you'll be okay. Stop struggling. It makes it worse."

37

LILLIA

I heard human sounds. The anguished screams were coming from something not of this earth, but from an angry, flaring figure, swirling above. A woman in a frayed black gown, tendrils of it twisting and knotting as she raged.

I watched Hank rise from the water, with Matt grasped in one hand. He reached back down and with a loud, deep yell, he pulled Charlie from the watery tomb with his other hand.

They all struggled to escape the water, but the raging figure swooped down and rushed toward them, pushing them back in. I knew they couldn't see her. They were frightened and confused. Pete raced to help rescue the boys.

This was the Pirate Queen Anne. I saw her in all her madness. Laurens wife, the watcher. I am with her.

I yelled above the noise and confusion. "Laurens sent

for me to help you, Anne. Please believe me." She spun to glare at me. "He wants you to end the watching. He loves you."

"No," she screamed. "Go away. All of you. My treasure is here. No one will ever take him."

I knew who she meant, her son Laurent…it had to be that. I pleaded, "Your treasure wasn't buried here. He lived. Your son lived."

Her hair whipped wildly as she spit out, "You lie," through her dry, cracked lips.

"He isn't here Anne. Laurent was rescued. He lived."

"How dare you speak his name." She cried, roaring up at the sky, "Your words cannot fool me. I know what you want. I know what they have all wanted. My treasure. My life."

I had to convince her! The poem said I would have the words. Poem? That's it! I screamed for Pete to come to me, hoping he could share this imagining. I needed him to help me speak the words.

"No Lillia, I need to get the boys and Hank to safety," he cried.

"The Pirate Queen is with us. She's going to kill the boys. We can't stop her until she knows her son is alive. She thinks he was buried here."

"What are you talking about?"

"Please, take my hand, there's no more time! Can you remember the poem on your wall?"

He clasped my hand in his and gasped. "Oh my Lord, now I can see her... what a beautiful woman."

"She needs to hear the poem from your wall."

Anne pushed close, her voice low and angry. "Go now. I've warned you."

I took a breath and started, "When you hear this mother, I don't..."

Pete's eyes misted over as he said as loudly and clearly as he could, "I don't know where I'll be. The words said by another, but know they come from me."

Anne spun in anger and lashed at him with a dagger pulled from her sash.

Pete ducked, stood back up, and with no fear in his voice repeated, "When you hear this mother, I don't know where I'll be. The words said by another, but know they come from me."

Her eyes burned with her anger. "I will kill you all!"

Pete, with unbelievable calm said, "A simple little rhyme, you often said for fun. You spoke this many a time, sweet whispers to your son."

Charlie coughed up water. Matt and Hank helped him. They were limping away toward the boat.

Anne saw them and let out a scream. "Stop! No!" She threw back her head. The wind roared around them.

I clung tighter to Pete's hand. We stood together. I prayed she would listen.

Pete shouted above the wind rush, "I love you madly..."

A low moan came from Anne. His words were getting

through to her. I squeezed Pete's hand. He was doing it. He was making her understand.

"...and forever."

Her screams stopped. Her eyes bore down on him.

"You know this to be so."

Her body shuddered. She watched.

"So I will leave you never..."

I saw her lips part. Then she whispered the last words together with Pete, "…And you must never go."

In the gentlest of gestures, Anne reached out toward Pete. He never wavered, just stayed standing tall, as she touched his cheek and swirled around him before disappearing.

I let out the breath I had been holding. "She knows now. You proved that he lived."

Tears welled in Pete's eyes. "'Somehow her son became part of my family. Thank God he lived to remember and record those words from his mother. The words she had whispered to her little boy. And that those words made their way through hundreds of years to this moment. Thank God."

38

MISSING

Nora and Cecelia didn't find anyone at Pete's house. They walked around his place searching for any sign of Lillia or the boys.

Pete's boss, Ray, came walking over from the direction of the seafood processing plant. "Hi Cecelia. You trying to find Pete too?"

"We are. Is he at work?"

"Nope. Should be though. Pete called in saying he might be late, but now I'm concerned. This isn't like him. Plus, his boat is gone. I hope he didn't get in trouble on the river. But it's odd, his bicycle is missing too."

"I think he may have gone out searching for my grandson and his friend," Cecelia said. "Here, take my phone number and I'll take yours. We'll call each other if anyone sees them."

"Sounds good. Hope he turns up soon," Ray said, as he headed back to work.

Nora said, "Aren't you worried? It seems they've been gone so long."

Cecelia patted her arm in an understanding way. "Matt's very responsible and Pete probably knows where they went and will find them. Come on, nothing more we can do here. Let's get back to the party."

Ahead the lights of the big house glowed. On the front verandah, the historical society group had gathered. Nora was so appreciative and happy that they decided to throw her a farewell party, but her stomach was in a knot. She wasn't going to be able to enjoy the wonderful food and friendship until she knew the kids were all safe.

"Any luck?" Myra asked when Nora and Cecelia joined her on the verandah.

"Nope, but they'll turn up," Cecelia said.

"Nora, while you were gone, a sweet little old lady dropped this off for Lillia. She said she was part of a painting class held here." Myra handed Nora a small canvas. "She pointed out that she had painted Lillia gazing out the window of the antique room. See her, right there?"

"Now wasn't that nice?" Nora leaned in closer to peer at the painting. "Looks like there are other people in the room too."

Myra saw what Nora was talking about. "That's odd. I gave Lillia permission to go in the room. But no one else was in the house at the time. We were closed."

Nora was getting more anxious. Something was up with Lillia. Those people in the room with her, what were they doing there? Who were they? And where was Lillia?

39

LILLIA

I gathered up Charlie...hugging him close. He was wet, cold, trembling. "It'll be all right. Let's get you out of here."

Hank stood nearby, his arms wrapped tight around his son. He looked over Matt's head toward me and mouthed the words *thank you*. I knew he realized how close he had come to losing his true treasure.

"What happened Pa?" Matt asked. "Charlie and I were just going to dig around a little and then everything went crazy."

Pete started to chuckle. "Well, this is one fine how do you do. Lillia here says we gotta find Charlie because he's supposed to be at a farewell party. So I figure, okay, I'll take the boat out and help her search. Next thing you know we see the three of you splashing around in this old backwater gunk."

"And Pa drops out of a tree," Matt said. "What was that about?"

Pretty soon we were all laughing, at what I wasn't quite sure, but it felt good

"Glad you were here," Matt said.

Hank gave Matt another hug and said, "Let's get out of here and back home to dry off." He reached out to shake Pete's hand. "Glad you decided to come out and find us. Appears these two treasure hunters are not the best swimmers."

Matt shoulder-bumped Hank, smiled up at him and said, "Hey, I can swim just fine! It was so weird, like I was being pushed under. What was making that happen?"

Hank shrugged his shoulders. "Don't ask me son. I sure as heck can't figure it out."

Pete said, "Bet the ground was slippery and you just sort of slid right in. These old waters can act up too. It's almost like the muddy bottom sucks you down. You get stuck in it. Just glad everyone lived to tell of it."

Great story Pete! Thinking quick on your feet. I would have to thank him for helping keep my imagining a secret.

The first words Charlie said were, "There's buried treasure here isn't there?"

I said, "Now Charlie, I'm not…"

Pete interrupted me with a wave of his hand and said, "That may just be true." He put his arm around Charlie and started walking toward the boats. I heard Pete telling Charlie about the tales he'd heard of a Pirate Queen watching her treasure site somewhere near Bon Secour. Hank and Matt followed. Hank's arm never left his son's shoulder.

I was grateful to Pete for the distraction as I went to gather the boy's shovels. I shook my head. Just like my little brother to leave a mess for me to pick up.

Beyond, about thirty feet into the forest, I saw a tall blonde man walking away. He was holding hands with a beautiful woman. He looked back at me and with a small smile, slight nod, and wink of his eye they were gone.

40

TREASURE FOUND

Waves and shouts came from the river bank as the two boats motored in.

Hank and Matt pulled alongside the dock. Captain Jack grabbed their boat and tied it on a piling. "Welcome back. I've been looking for you."

Hank cringed, thinking not that again. Then, realizing Jack meant he was looking for Matt and not him, he breathed a sigh of relief. The idea of people always looking for him because he owed them something was not a good feeling. He thought, I'm never going to let my son, my treasure, be disappointed in me again.

Matt said, "We're glad to be back."

Jack laughed and said, "Looks like you all had quite a day. Swimming? Don't know if this is the right time, but I wanted to make sure you knew I was serious about that job offer.

Matt stepped out onto the dock. "Let me just say that if you hire me to help with the Pirate Adventure Cruise, I'll have a good story of my own to tell the tourists."

"Hoping you can start tomorrow."

Matt reached out to shake Jack's hand. "I'd be happy to sail with you Captain!"

Hank beamed and smiled at Matt, saying, "Proud of you boy."

Pete brought his boat up the dock and climbed out after Lillia and Charlie.

Lillia said, "Thanks, Pete. I owe you one."

"No problem. Glad to help," Pete replied. "Oh no, the boss is here."

Ray came striding over. "Hey there. You're late aren't you?"

"Ah, yes sir I am. A bit of an emergency to take care of."

His boss took in the motley crew standing on the dock and said, "I guess I can overlook it as it seems you might have been part of a rescue mission? Job well done Pete! Looks like you have a bunch of friends here to welcome you back." He pointed to the group coming down the old road from the big house.

Nora raced up to Lillia and Charlie.

Charlie started talking the moment he saw her. "Graun-tie, we found a buried treasure site. Pete said the ghost of the pirate lady was trying to scare us away. She was protecting her son I guess. But not really? Pete had a poem, like a prayer I think. Anyway he read it over the place. So now it's safe to go back there and dig up the treasure chest."

Nora said, "Slow down Charlie. First things first. Come here and hug your old Grauntie. You gave me quite a scare. Everyone here was so worried."

Cecelia ran to hug Matt.

Matt said, "Grannie, Pa saved us from drowning."

Cecelia couldn't believe her ears. Matt almost drowned? And his father actually saved him? She glanced up toward heaven and blew a kiss to her daughter.

Hank, with hope in his eyes, said, "Miss Cecelia, can you forgive me? I haven't been much of a father to Matt."

"I can Hank, if you can forgive me for being so hard on you," Cecelia answered.

Matt thought this was the best day he'd had in a long time. Even if he almost drowned! A job, Pa and Grannie being nice to each other. Couldn't ask for more.

Charlie took Grauntie by the hand and walked over to Pete. "Pete, can you show us that poem you were reciting over the burial site? The one you said settled the spirits down?"

"Sure, come on in y'all. I've got some other things to show you too," Pete said, waving for everyone to follow.

A shout came from down the road. It was Myra scurrying along, with a family trying to keep up with her.

"Hey wait up, I've been worried too. Is everyone okay?" Myra called out.

Jack gave a big wave. "Why look, it's that nice family from the tour the other day."

41

LILLIA

I was surprised to see Tod and his family again!

Tod's dad said to me, "Sorry to have missed the house tours, but we saw the lights on and thought we might catch you to say goodbye and wish you well. You and your brother were so nice helping with the children on the cruise."

The twins ran up and hugged my legs. Tod hung back, but gave me that great smile of his.

"And then we found ourselves visiting with your grandaunt and her friends," the mom said. "So here we are. Oh and look, there's Captain Jack."

More volunteers walked toward us to see what was going on. Seemed like most of the party had shifted down to the river. They followed Pete inside to see his mini museum.

Grauntie pulled me aside and said, "Lillia, are you all

right? Did something happen out there besides just falling in the river?"

I thought about how much more to say. So far only Pete knew what really happened. Of course, Hank and the boys had their suspicions, but I think I could get out of saying a whole lot more to them. Pete seemed to be handling their questions just fine.

I liked the idea that Charlie, Matt and Hank heard Pete recite the verses, but didn't see the Pirate Queen. Somehow they accepted that he had cleared her out of the area. I liked staying in the background.

Now what to say to Grauntie. I decided to simply tell her that it had been an interesting day and maybe we'd talk about it later. She gave me that sideways stare of hers and said, "Your decision. Just so I know you're okay."

"I'm fine Grauntie. Let's go to Pete's house. You should see it. Like a museum."

Everyone had crowded in to admire Pete's ship models and see all the memorabilia he had.

I heard Myra say, "Why Pete Gavin, you have a treasure trove here. I'd like to discuss the Baldwin County Historical Society meeting with you and looking at what you've acquired. Perhaps we can work out some joint tours? Does that interest you? I hope you'll say yes."

"That sounds like a wonderful idea. Maybe I could do some story telling about the ships that came to this landing in its heyday."

"Sounds like you have some great ideas!" Myra said.

I was happy for Pete. All the work he'd put into this collection would be rewarded.

Charlie said, "And if you go back and find treasure, you could put it here too."

"Treasure?" Myra asked.

"On a channel of the river near the mystery fort," Charlie said.

Myra tapped her finger on her lips. "Hmm, I know the land donated to the society extends into those backwaters. So if there was buried treasure it would belong to the Historical Society. It sure would help with maintenance and support for the house."

"Since Pete got rid of the mean old Pirate Queen we could head back to search for it," Hank said.

Cecelia rolled her eyes and shook her head.

Hank saw her, laughed and winked before saying, "Don't worry Miss Cecelia, I've learned 'bout real treasure today and I've got all I'll ever be needing. Just saying, I'll help if y'all decide to look for it."

Cecelia smiled. "Something sure straightened him out in those backwaters today," she whispered to me.

I said, "I agree with you!"

Tod came by to say his family was leaving. "If you ever get to South Dakota, here's my phone number. I'd be happy to show you around."

I waved good bye to them.

I exchanged my good byes with Pete. He was excited about the idea of sharing his knowledge with others. I was grateful he had come with me today. I would never have remembered the verses his ancestor wrote all those years ago.

Matt and Hank were heading home with Cecelia. They looked good together…happy.

Ahead of me Charlie was chatting to Myra, sharing his excitement about the adventure he'd had. It was hard to imagine what would have happened if we hadn't gotten there in time.

"Lillia, come on now. Time to head out," Grauntie said.

"Okay. Where is that cabin you're going to this fall?"

"It's in the Black Hills area of South Dakota honey," she answered. "I hope you decide to join me for a few days."

"I think I will," I said.

I walked up toward the mansion with Grauntie. In the upstairs window a candle was burning. The girls were home.

If any of you ever visit the Swift-Coles house in Bon Secour, pause in that upstairs hallway, close your eyes, and say hello to them from me.

ABOUT THE AUTHOR

The Swift-Coles Historic Home in Bon Secour, Alabama is open for guided tours. Please take the opportunity to visit it.

For photographs of the area, and historic photographs of the real Swift family, please visit my website.

There you will also find links to my Facebook, Instagram, Pinterest, and YouTube social media sites.

I look forward to hearing from readers! I'd love to receive photographs of you reading *Watched Places* or visiting Alabama.

Happy reading…
Brenda Felber

www.pameroymystery.com
brenda@brendafelber.com

84809087R00109

Made in the USA
Columbia, SC
18 December 2017